THE ROPE AROUND YOUR WAIST

THE ROPE
AROUND
YOUR WAIST

Fellie Oka Moh

RESOURCE *Publications* · Eugene, Oregon

THE ROPE AROUND YOUR WAIST

Resource Publications
An Imprint of Wipf and Stock Publishers
199 W. 8th Ave., Suite 3
Eugene, OR 97401

www.wipfandstock.com

PAPERBACK ISBN: 978-1-7252-9170-6
HARDCOVER ISBN: 978-1-7252-9171-3
EBOOK ISBN: 978-1-7252-9172-0

04/12/21

To Emmanuel Nnamdi Moh who leaves physical
and psychological spaces for me to dream and sing

Contents

CHAPTER 1

Adaugo in crisis

WE SET OFF EARLY THAT SATURDAY MORNING, LEAVING AS EARLY AS 6 AM.
The journey from Rumuimo to Okiti will take approximately four hours
and we had to return the same day. In the vehicle were my father, mother,
two of my brothers, and myself. One of my brothers was driving. We packed
our breakfast and lunch in food warmers. The chill harmattan air, added to
the fog, made visibility difficult at first. Rumuimo harmattan was as severe
as its rainy season. When the rains came, it was as if the skies had quota of
rainwater which they must exhaust daily. Just a few hours of rainfall was
enough to turn the entire town into one muddy puddle. We picked our way
through the barely visible roads as we moved out of town.

The harmattan haze didn't deter the policemen from performing their
civic duties. Driving through the numerous police checkpoints, one would
think that we were passing through war zones, but they weren't actually
checking anything. Money just exchanged hands between the policemen
and the public transporters who hailed these security agents and moved on.
It didn't matter whether they were carrying a gang of robbers, or the vehicle
was dangerously overloaded or was not even roadworthy to start with. They
didn't have to stop us. The presence of my parents in the Peugeot 504 station wagon was an insurance against any suspicion of reckless driving. So
when some of the policemen stopped us for routine checks, they greeted
my parents respectfully, solicited for their blessings, and waved us off.

We weren't talking much among ourselves. This was unlike other family travels when there would be lively chatter as we relived past experiences.

All it would take was for someone to say "remember when," and the laughter would commence. But on this particular trip, no one felt inclined to talk. The calmness and quietness in the car were a sharp contrast to the discomfort we all felt.

Two hours into our journey, my mother's maternal instinct told her we were hungry and needed breakfast. She suddenly instructed my brother to stop at a filling station. We came out and used their conveniences. I was in no mood for breakfast, but I knew that she wasn't going to listen. So I accepted my assigned portion and ate absentmindedly. The short break and food was good for my brother who was driving. We set off once more.

We arrived Okiti on schedule. As we entered the village, I could count the number of young people I met on the roads on my fingertips. Okiti wasn't the Nollywood typical village of mud houses, large farms, and thick forests. There was no evil forest because the people had long embraced Christianity. It had an impressive collection of modern houses, a beautiful primary school, and a health center. Yet, it was shunned by the young and the healthy who preferred to live in the rowdy townships, abandoning the village for the elderly. It was only during the annual 'migration' of Igbos during the Christmas festivities that the town would be bustling with life. Why build a mansion in the village which was used for about ten days in a year? Such people lived as tenants in overcrowded urban flats. There were many things I couldn't understand.

Entering my husband's compound, my eyes caught sight of the coconut and kolanut trees. My parents had given the saplings to my in-laws to plant in my honor as I got married. That was six years ago. They had sprouted but were not yet mature trees. I noticed that someone had set fire on the grass surrounding the two trees. Parts of the leaves were charred, a yellowish-green, but the stems appeared unaffected.

Lady mother-in-law welcomed us. Her face was expressionless. In the sitting room was my husband, his uncle, Nwagbo, and one younger brother. I was glad that we didn't meet a crowded village of elders. We were keeping our misunderstanding within the family. Uncle Nwagbo was my favorite among his uncles. I could tell from the beginning, before marrying Chukwudi, that he loved me. Every wife can sense where she stands with each of her in-laws. There is always that in-law that wholeheartedly accepts and loves you. There is the one that doesn't like you and won't bother trying to hide the fact that you're not as beautiful, as young or as brilliant as they would have liked. Bottom-line is that their brother is too good for you and

2

you should consider yourself lucky making such a good catch. There is also the in-law that's not bothered about your existence. Uncle Nwagbo was a reasonable man with a great family of his own.

I searched my husband's face for emotions, but it was bland and uncommunicative. Chukwudi's mother tried to offer us breakfast, but my father politely declined on our behalf. We had eaten on the way and we were not hungry.

Without much ado, he went straight to the discussion.

"We noticed that Adaugo hasn't been looking too well. We thought she was sick, but she assured us it was nothing of the kind. Four days ago, she drove into the house when we were about to sleep. She told us some things. We allowed her to rest for a few days and we have brought her back to her husband's family. In every marriage, there must be some misunderstanding. A snake seen by only one person is described as a python, so we don't buy only her side of the story. My son, let us know what the matter is. We may be able to help you sort out your issues and the marriage will continue as before."

He ended his speech and waited. After a long pause, Chukwudi responded.

"Thanks for making this trip. Please, believe whatever your daughter told you about me. If you like, feel free to add your own. I had determined that no outside person will settle any case between me and the woman that I marry. The day that happens is the end of the marriage. I didn't send your daughter out of my house. She cursed me bitterly and left. For her to curse me in such an abominable manner and to leave my house without my chasing her out shows she's no more interested in the marriage. That is my decision and it is final."

Uncle Nwagbo cleared his throat.

"My son," he began, "you don't throw away the baby with the dirty water. Women can say anything when they are angry. You don't just have yourselves to think about but the happiness of your two children."

"Why didn't she think of them? Is she not their mother? What of the curse that she placed on me? Which mother curses the father of her children in such a manner?" he interjected.

"But you can't just end your marriage because your wife said some things to you in anger. Did she steal in the market square? Did you catch her with another man? Did she abuse your mother? People don't just end their marriages for frivolous reasons. Remember what happened to Nwokedi," his uncle warned.

Nwokedi's story was well-known in the community. He married the daughter of one of the rich men in the town. She had two little children for him when he told her they were traveling to the village. He took her straight to her family and announced that he wasn't marrying her any longer; her rich father should marry her. The elders gathered to settle the issue. He said his anger was because he wanted her to get the children ready for them to go to a photographer's studio for a family portrait and she refused. The elders inquired from him if she didn't go in the end? But, she eventually agreed and they went for it. The elders continued to listen. For refusing to go when he mentioned it at first, she was a rebellious arrogant wife who was counting on her father's wealth and he didn't want the marriage any more. The elders pleaded and the young wife wept but he refused to listen. With tears she told him, 'Nwokedi, if any woman lives with you as a wife for one year at a stretch, then everybody will know that I am indeed a bad woman.' True to her words, Nwokedi had remarried about five times and none of the marriages lasted up to a year.

My father raised the question of my children.

"Chukwudi, while we give you time to re-think your position, we will beg that you let Adaugo keep the two little girls. You see, they are still young and they will best be cared for by their mother. Even the courts will award custody of such young children to their mother. Please don't separate them," my father pleaded.

"Thanks once again," Chukwudi responded. "I am the father of Ify and Somto unless somebody proves me wrong. My children will stay with me and me only. Even the courts cannot award custody to her if they know that she's not mentally stable to take care of them. I am ready to fight this battle to its logical conclusion, but my children remain with me."

"What evidence do you have to show that she's not stable?" my father asked.

"Who curses her husband in such an abominable manner?" he responded.

"She spoke in anger and we can sort this out," Uncle Nwagbo defended me.

My father and his uncle were appealing for calm, but I could see that Chukwudi's mind was made up. I looked at Lady Mother-in-law to see where she stood. I could see that she wasn't just on her son's side but that she was very angry with me.

While the discussions were going on, I noticed that she was preparing for her drama. I thought this woman loved me. She had received me so warmly when Chukwudi brought me for introduction. She removed the light blue branded t-shirt that she was wearing over the half faded wrapper she wore for doing household chores. My eyes idly went to the inscription on the back of the t-shirt: 'Adieu Papa! We shall surely miss you.' Yes. A souvenir from a family burial. The type that is worn by nearly the whole village to give the deceased patriarch a befitting burial.

Oh, back to Chukwudi's mother. In what looked like a scene in a Nollywood movie, she had unstrapped her bra too. Cupping her sagging breasts, breasts that had been dealt mortal blows by the suckling of her eight children, she moved towards Chukwudi.

"If you know you sucked these breasts, you must never marry this wicked woman again. Unless you didn't suck these breasts . . .."

She continued with the unnecessary blackmail. They were already in each other's confidences.

Chukwudi lowered his head. Even if he wished to backtrack from his earlier trenchant attitude, with this tacit support, he dared not lift his gaze to confront her. Whatever he said now will be used against him. If he continued to keep quiet, Mama will count it as insolence, after all, silence is the best answer to a fool. If he answered, he was still insolent. How dare he answer his mother who carried him for nine months, and went through hell to raise him?

The entire story of her privations and tribulations as a widow had been told him ad nauseam. It all came out again. "When your father died and I was left alone with eight of you to raise, nobody lent me a helping hand. I sold my wrapper to pay your WAEC fees. What did I not do? I fried and sold akara; I farmed, I did daily jobs hired by the rich, to bring food home. I fought to make my first son a man. He gets a job and marries this woman who is pouring curses on him. If you don"t promise me that you won't marry her again, I will kill myself and my blood will be on your head."

This last threat got to my mother. This reconciliatory meeting wasn't going as envisaged. The tension that made me move back home was escalating quickly.

Communication had broken down completely between Chukwudi and me. I didn't want to join the statistics of physically abused wives. The level of anger Chukwudi was showing was frightening. I had heard of husbands killing their wives in a fit of anger; an action which they had the luxury of spending whatever remained of their meaningless lives to regret.

So when I saw the flashes of anger, I loaned myself sense and went back to my parents. But divorce or separation is not part of the marriage deal where I come from. Once married you must remain married.

"Marriage takes patience, my daughter."

"A wise woman will manage and control even the most foolish of men."

"Don't let another woman snatch your husband."

This last one always made me laugh. Were the men so truly foolish and indecisive that a cunning woman could simply snatch him as a toy from his careless wife? I couldn't credit my father or brothers with such irresponsibility and indiscretion. If I have sons, I would raise them to be real men; to take decisions by themselves and to take responsibility for their choices, instead of blaming their innocent wives for their moral failures. It struck me! I wasn't going to have sons. My marriage had just collapsed and one bad marriage was enough to last me a lifetime.

My parents were not giving up yet. This visit was their idea to ensure that we got back on track together. It was agreed that both families should sit down with us and help us to iron out our differences.

My father was particularly worried. If my marriage collapsed he would be stripped of all his titles. He would be judged as a failed father who had not succeeded in raising a responsible child. He wanted peace at all cost.

But my mother wanted the welfare of her child, inside or outside marriage.

An observer looking at her dressing to the meeting will think that it was a National Party of Political Thugs meeting that she was going for. She wore knee-length shorts, a t-shirt, and a pair of boots.

As Lady Mother-in-law was showcasing the breasts that will silence her son and ensure that he doesn't compromise on his earlier stand, my mother got up.

"I gave birth to Adaugo and shortly after, the Biafran Civil War started. Malnutrition didn't kill her! Wild animals didn't kill her! Soldiers' bullets didn't kill her! The bombs didn't kill her! I want to tell you, Chukwudi and your mother; a husband will not kill my daughter. Get up, let's go. They are no more interested in the marriage."

I looked at my husband, Chukwudi. His gaze was still on the ground. I looked at my two brothers. They came to the meeting battle-ready. I guess they were just waiting for the slightest sign of violence to pounce on my husband and give him the beating of his life. They were very angry with him. Even though I reassured them over and over that he had not physically abused me, they couldn't believe what made me come down from a seventy-five kg weight to fifty-fivekg. I had lost so much weight that I was ashamed of answering the questions of friends and acquaintances. I had resorted to lying. 'Oh, so you didn't hear that I was ill? I was hospitalized. But thank God I'm getting better now.'

I couldn't lie to my family. The marriage was weighing me down. I was scared.

I am a jovial and friendly person. Chukwudi knows that, and so he exploited it as an instrument of torture. He could stay one full week without talking to me. I was dying inside.

I was also insecure and vulnerable. I had two daughters for him. Will he diss me and look for a lady who would give him the almighty sons? When the pressure became unbearable, I moved out on my own. I needed to get back my life, first.

But maybe I shouldn't have threatened him the way I did, which was the reason for his Mom's behavior.

"I said let's go." It was my mother's voice.

I looked at Chukwudi again. It seemed like a dream. My super loving husband. My knight in shining armor. The one who had promised me 'no beating no cheating.'

Our marriage had begun with so much promise. So much optimism. We were to be the S_1 Unit for measuring happy couples. We were going to be so happy that if happiness was a person, it would be envious of us. We were in love. We had looked down on other couples that were having issues and felt secure that our relationship was immune from crashing. Our dreams, such beautiful dreams! They got married and lived happily ever after! Was this the 'happily ever after?' With Chukwudi's mother sticking her breasts in his face and my mother answering her retort with retort?

I waited for a little time. Darling husband, say something. Tell your mother to control her outbursts. Tell my mother that you are sorry. Come to me. Tell me there's a mistake somewhere and I am dreaming about this nightmare.

He kept looking at the ground.

No, I won't cry. Have I not wept enough?

I picked up what was left of my battered dignity; I followed my family and we left.

CHAPTER 2

Nkechi, Adaugo's mother

WHICH MOTHER CAN FORGET THE DAY SHE GAVE BIRTH TO HER CHILD, especially her first child? Just a month after my wedding, I missed my period. Despite the threat of the Civil War hanging over our heads like an ominous cloud, my husband was ecstatic.

"It's going to be a boy. He will be a striker in football, just like his father. Or maybe, we will train him to become a medical doctor or an engineer."

"Or a lawyer," I added. "What if it's a girl? Will you be disappointed?"

"If it's a girl, you've just got yourself a rival. It means that God is so good to me. I marry one pretty girl and get another for free."

Times were hard, but we were optimistic that the war will not happen or even if it happened, it won't last. He bought me a live chicken to celebrate the conception.

Where I come from, everybody values a fertile womb, and nothing satisfies the womb watchers as seeing a bride fall pregnant if possible on her wedding night.

Everywhere I went, I met approving eyes and quiet whispers. I could read the unspoken words: you're a good girl; you kept yourself from premarital sex. If a woman is chaste, she will find it easy to conceive. But if there's a delay even by one day, it must be the result of the numerous abortions that she had committed as a girl.

My young husband was walking about with pride. His steps announced to anyone who cared to notice that he is a real man. Fertile and virile, he was already considered successful in the community. He had graduated from the university, secured a good government job, rented a two-bedroom apartment, bought a small car, and married a wife. Now he was going to be a father and has earned the right to be respected as a responsible and successful man. I was proud of him and all his achievements. He had told me that before long, we would move to our house and stop calling anybody 'landlord.'

I was pampered. Every woman who had gone through pregnancy and delivery had a piece of advice for me. Each gave a list of what I may or may not eat, how I should or shouldn't lie down, and how often or rarely I should have sex with my husband. Pregnancy is a communal experience and everybody was involved.

I told my husband about the sex embargo.

"The older women say we must keep off each other for a minimum of five months to avoid a miscarriage."

"Go and tell whoever told you that your husband is a very healthy male. Unless she's suggesting that I marry another woman."

"God forbid!" I spat out.

Being pregnant was good. I could ask for anything and my husband would rush to provide it. I wasn't just making up the strange desires. It appears the hormones were wreaking havoc on my taste buds. I didn't enjoy the meals I cooked by myself, so he was going frequently to other women to collect food for his pregnant wife. They indulged him with smiles.

"Is that what the baby wants?"

The older and more experienced women regaled me with stories of labor and delivery. The optimists talked of waking up from sleep to find the baby lying by their side; climbing a tree and looking down to see the baby crying on the ground; going to the toilet and easing out the baby just like that. All these sounded too good to be true.

At a point, I felt that the pessimists were on a free race to outdo one another on the horrifying stories they shared. One described being in labor for seven consecutive days. How was it possible to be in pain for seven straight days and stay alive to tell the story? She told me I should prepare my mind for the worst. Another woman told of the baby coming out with the legs first. In forcing the baby out, the midwife decapitated the baby. Still, another told of how she bled until she fainted. The doctors gave her blood transfusion and it took her six months to return to her normal life. I heard of postpartum depression. Demon attack, they called it. One of my in-laws, fine woman, would be perfectly normal throughout pregnancy. Once she was delivered of the baby, the trouble would start. She won't know where her baby is. She won't eat by herself. She would sit staring into space and crying intermittently for nearly four months after delivery. The family would take her to doctors, both orthodox and native, but next pregnancy, it would recur. Horrifying to say the least. I heard of retained placenta that led to severe bleeding that killed the new mothers. I heard of multiple births, twins, and triplets that produced dead babies.

I became scared. I didn't want to be pregnant again. I began wishing for a miscarriage. I repeated the horror stories to my husband. I was afraid of dying in labor. I didn't want to die young. He always reassured me that nothing but good will happen to me. But the comfort was always short-lived. I was having nightmares where headless babies were pursuing me in my dreams. I would wake up drenched in sweat.

I admired women who had gone through pregnancy several times and survived with their babies. These mothers are unsung heroines. I had looked forward to motherhood, but I didn't know that there was this level of anxiety that accompanied the process. I was afraid of having deformed or imbecilic babies. I dreaded twins or triplets too because I heard that many were born pre-term and underweight and would need special care to survive. Where will I get such care? It had better be one baby at a time.

I bought every book I could lay hands on that explained the process of conception. I read all the sections on pregnancy and delivery many times. I read some of the books so many times that I could quote whole passages off memory. Knowledge is true power. I felt better getting as much information as was necessary.

Nausea! Oh, nausea! How can one describe the carbide taste in the mouth? It was as if a malevolent creature was playing pranks with the contents of my stomach through my nostrils. Every pleasant fragrance had been distorted into irritation. I threw up easily, sometimes, without warning. It was difficult to hold down anything, even water, for the first three months. I was certain that I was going to be sick forever.

Twelve weeks later, the nausea I was experiencing disappeared as suddenly as it had started. It was like going to bed sick and waking up without a single trace of disease. My appetite returned. I ate better and looked healthier. By then the Civil War had started but it was still sounding like a faraway event from where we lived.

I had a healthy pregnancy and a surprisingly 'easy' labor for a first-time mother. The 'easy' was by the assessment of the midwives. As for me, there was nothing easy about having contractions which increased in intensity and frequency from eight in the morning till six in the evening when the baby arrived.

How can one adequately explain the last moments of labor? The searing pain! The plain unspeakable anguish! The resolutions never to go near any man again! The anger that the punishment on the woman is undeserved! I cursed my husband and the unjust assignment of punishment. The midwife talked of the bag of waters breaking. I don't know what happened but I felt warm liquid rush down my thighs even though I was not urinating. Then came the indescribable pain as I felt something pressing with force against my lower pelvis. It seemed I would be split into two. I later heard that I was given a 'cut,' but I didn't know when or how. I couldn't localize the pain because it appeared my whole body up to my brain was on fire. I heard the midwife screaming at me to push. I tried with whatever little strength I had to obey, but it wasn't enough. She slapped me roughly on my thigh.

"Push out this baby or you want all your suffering to be in vain."

I heard her, and with all my might, I pushed. Something slipped out of me. The pains disappeared. I was peaceful and calm. So I am a mother! I closed my eyes and began thanking God.

Those days, ultrasound machines were not available, so the sex of the baby was known and announced only at the point of delivery. One of the birth attendants took the good news to my waiting, anxious husband.

"Your wife won. It is a girl."

He was ecstatic! He ran round in a frenzy for some seconds before he sobered up suddenly.

"What of my wife? Is the placenta out? I hope she's not bleeding too much?"

He was assured that I was good, but he wasn't satisfied until baby and I had been cleaned up and brought into our sitting room. He held his daughter in his arms and I saw tears of joy in his eyes. He called her Adaugo (the daughter of an eagle).

It wasn't quite up to six weeks later that the war reached us at Rumuimo and we left the town to seek safety in remote farmlands. My husband left us to enlist in the army. Here I was, a first-time mother with a tiny baby, left to fend for myself and her. I would hear airplanes overhead and dash for cover. We lived in thatched houses that let in rain during the rainy season. Occasionally the winds blew off the palm fronds and my daughter and I would huddle in a corner, shivering with cold and fear.

I saw mothers throwing away their children while running for their dear life. I saw malnourished children who were left by their fleeing mothers to die. I remember a child shrieking out to the mother:

"Mama! Mama, don't leave me!"

But Mama needed to survive first. It was a heart-rending experience. I was afraid to think of what may have happened to my husband. I moved from one day to another like one in a trance and was grateful just to be alive. All around me were the sick, the hungry, and the dying. My daughter and I were severely malnourished and emaciated but we were not sick.

Salt was a scarce commodity. Fortunately, we discovered a salt lake close to one of the places we had erected makeshift structures. With the saline water, we were good, but we needed a lot of vegetables to reduce the salty taste. We ate any green leafy vegetables we saw to survive: waterleaf, *ugu*, cassava leaves, shrubs that I hadn't known were edible, we ate all. For protein, we ate crabs, rats, and whatever game we could catch. I joined other women to fish in the local rivers. The seafood supplemented our protein supply.

God bless the International Red Cross Society. They brought us beans, milk, stockfish, and drugs. They often attended to Adaugo and me, especially on those times when we were a few meals away from death by starvation. War is evil. Nobody should pray for such devastation. The Red Cross marked the fingers of the children for food rations based on their health status. Those who were severely malnourished had more fingers marked, indicating that they could go to the food distribution center more frequently than others.

Our temporary village had five of us mothers, but the others had more children. It's amazing the friendship and co-operation that existed among us. We were united by a zeal to live. We cooked together and encouraged one another. We wept together when we lost a child to kwashiorkor and rejoiced when someone survived a malaria attack. We survived.

On one beautiful day, we heard that the war had ended and we could return to our home towns. Adaugo was a three-year-old wild-eyed and inquisitive girl. I returned with joy and anxiety mixed. I couldn't tell if I was still married or had become a widow like many other young women. There was no means of communication except to wait. Soldiers that returned from the war front informed relatives of their comrades that had died. When we heard such news, the mourning followed. Mothers had lost sons.

Wives lost husbands and families had lost children. An elderly woman was informed that she had lost all her three adult sons. We all knew that she wouldn't survive the news. She should have just died in the farms instead of fighting to live just to face more sadness and anguish. She was found dead the following morning after the news.

Apart from death, some families had become irretrievably broken. A young man returned to hear that the wife he married shortly before the outbreak of the war had married a soldier and moved on. He immediately became a psychiatric case. The hope of reuniting with the love of his life was what kept him going through the three years' war. I thought that men managed their emotions better, but here was evidence that ultimately, we are all humans who can hurt badly!

Another returned and wasn't talking to anybody. He was just muttering to himself. I learned it was called shell shock. We hoped that with time, he would fully regain his senses. My brother-in-law returned, round with fat in wrong places and with glowing skin.

"Where did you fight your own war? Or you didn't fight at all?" I asked him.

"I was a cook for the soldiers. When they overran a village, they brought goats and chickens and I prepared the meals for them. I thoroughly enjoyed myself."

Different strokes! I'm sure he would have cared less if the war continued.

About ten days after our return, I saw him coming to the house. My husband was as lean as a rake. With his torn clothes, sunken eyes, and unfocused gaze, he could be mistaken for a mad man.

I let out a wild scream and threw myself at him. We fell on the ground. We were wailing together. Other returnees joined us in crying. A casual observer would think that somebody died. We sang, we laughed, and we praised God. A woman let out a loud ululation; the type that accompanies the birth of a baby boy. And the dancing started. There was no money to buy food or drinks to celebrate, but dancing was free. We were happy.

Chukwudi looked up and saw her. Adaugo was crying and pulling me to get up from the ground. My husband screamed with joy again.

"So she made it too! I feared that my daughter must have died of kwashiorkor. God, you love me so much."

He tried to carry her, but she screamed and ran away from him. We both smiled. She will come round.

Good food—the best we could wrack up—rest and change of clothes and my husband were back to his normal self. He returned to his job as a civil servant and I returned to mine as a teacher in one of the township schools. We were lucky that our house wasn't damaged during the war. It was as if we merely locked it up and traveled, and came back some years later. Others had to re-roof their houses that air raids had destroyed. Our landlord was alive and well too. Traders tried to return to their businesses but the purchasing power of people was limited. We returned to trading by barter and using cassava and salt as currencies. But our lives picked up quickly. Years later, we were able to move into our own house in a different part of town. Suburbs, it was called. But we were glad to live there.

Adaugo was the center of our lives and the source of continuous joy. Other children came, but she retained a special place as the child that had suffered most with me. Our bond was strong. She could tell me anything. Well, almost anything. I recollect her coming back from school in Primary Five to tell me that their teacher told them a secret which she said was for only girls. I called her into my room to listen.

"She said that when we get bigger, blood will start coming out of our private part once every month and our breasts will get big like women's breasts."

I wondered if such information wasn't too early to tell an eleven-year-old. But since the teacher had started it, I followed it up with 'the talk.' I patted myself for a job well done until we had another conversation. "Mommy, your tummy is big."

"I'm pregnant and I'm going to have another baby," I teased her.

"You can't be. You said it's a boy that does it to somebody." I laughed! So Daddy was just Daddy, he wasn't a boy.

Looks like I had more explanations to do.

"Ada, do let me know when you start seeing that blood."

She dutifully informed me of her first period in her thirteenth year. I had sworn I would enlighten my daughter on sex and relationships. All that my mother told me on my first period was 'If a boy touches you or plays with you, you'll be pregnant.'

So when I had my first period, I started avoiding my elder and younger brothers until Mama noticed. I had given my younger brother the beating of his life for trying to play with me. He was nine years old

"Why are you behaving so strangely?"

"It's because of what you told me that if a boy plays with me, I would get pregnant. Since he came back from school, he's been trying to play skipping games with me. I don't even know if I'm pregnant already." I was crying.

It became a joke in the whole family. My parents repeated the story to whoever cared to listen. They were pleased with my ignorance and innocence, but I didn't want my daughter to be that naïve. A twelve-year-old friend of mine was told by her mother. 'If they tell you to do, don't do.'

She wasn't told what it was that she shouldn't do. When she fell pregnant at fifteen, she had no idea what was happening.

So I told Adaugo about the sperm cell uniting with the egg to form a baby. Before I could proceed, she asked, "Where do they meet to form this baby?"

My husband who had been listening quickly beat a retreat and allowed me to hold this uncomfortable discussion all by myself. She wasn't done with the questions.

"The egg released by the woman, does it have a shell? Can one pick it out? Is it as big as a chicken egg?"

I answered the much I knew and told her that we would continue the discussions. We agreed that sex should be delayed till marriage and that she should feel free to report any case of sexual harassment to me and it would be treated in confidentiality. I taught her proper hygiene and how to use sanitary towels. I bought her roll-on deodorants and a fancy wristwatch for attaining the status of a 'fellow woman.'

I thought that we had a good confidential chat until I saw her younger brother shifting uneasily while talking to me.

"What's that?" I asked him.

"The sanitary towel I put under my briefs wants to fall off," he told me innocently.

"Why would you wear a sanitary towel?" I was struggling to control my laughter.

"I saw Adaugo wearing it to keep her pants clean. So I decided to try it."

I had anticipated some rebellion as she entered teenage. I had heard of the turbulent teens. The only cause of concern was discovering Chukwudi's love letters to her when she was in senior secondary school. I had brought her back from the boarding house and was going through her stuff when I saw the letters with the heart-shaped signs on them. I felt a sickening fear. Teenage pregnancy, sexually transmitted diseases, the reputation of being a wayward girl. My mind jumped from one frightening scenario to another. I was disappointed that she hadn't taken me into confidence as we had agreed.

"My friends said you don't tell Mommies such things." She was making excuses for herself.

"But who loves you more? Mommy or your friends? Who will be there for you if anything should go wrong? Who will defend you and protect you?" I wanted my daughter to know that the penalty for promiscuous lifestyle was heavy and the major and greatest dividends were paid by the woman.

I threatened to take her to a doctor to conduct a virginity test. She had insisted that the relationship was in all purity, but I told her that I couldn't believe her until she was tested. "When can we go, Mom? I'm telling you the truth. Take me to a doctor, if that will give you peace of mind and convince you that I am saying the truth and nothing but the truth."

I looked at my daughter's earnest face, and I believed her. When he was eventually told, my husband wanted to make a mountain of this mole-hill, but I assured him that such a reaction was extreme. Which growing girl doesn't have an admirer? And who said that all such crushes led to sex? I had my own teenage crush. The intense affection lasted for about three months and fizzled out. When I saw him later, I was wondering if his head had always been so big and why were his legs so spindly?

Even though I acted harshly, I was actually flattered that my daughter was already having serious admirers who didn't want to 'chop and clean mouth' but wanted marriage. But my daughter's future came first. I did more of 'the talk' with her, painting vivid pictures of the heavy price of an immoral lifestyle. Teenage pregnancy, diseases, and a loss of focus on academics and career were great prices to pay for what one could have later in life. We put down our feet and the relationship was nipped in the bud. Or so I thought.

They say the first cut is the deepest. She would later present Chukwudi as a suitor. Her love for him, though latent and suppressed, was still waxing strong. I saw my daughter glowing. I saw she was happy with her choice and I was satisfied. What else could a mother ask for, if not her child's happiness? We did our background checks on Chukwudi and his family and we didn't hear any unpleasant details. No mental ill-health and no kleptomania. We supported their marriage.

Everything seemed to go well for some years. Adaugo and Chukwudi made me a joyful grandmother. I called him my son-in-love and not a son-in-law. Then gradually I started noticing changes. Chukwudi was getting withdrawn from us. He had always considered us as his parents, but that was beginning to change. I tried to find out from Adaugo, but she was discreet about the happenings in her home. They didn't want parental interference.

Adaugo was losing weight at a frightening rate, but she still insisted that she was alright and that we shouldn't worry. But her father was anxious.

"Don't you think you should call your daughter and have a deep conversation with her? Maybe she has a terminal illness and she doesn't want us to know yet."

"I have tried but she's not opening up to me. Maybe Chukwudi has been unfaithful and infected her with HIV/ AIDS."

We wept at the prospect. I couldn't but worry. The umbilical cord binding me to my daughter was physically severed at birth, but I could still feel it tugging at my heart. Following my husband's suggestions, I recommended medical tests but she told me they were unnecessary. She had neither breast cancer nor HIV/AIDS.

"I think she's being abused at home," was my husband's conclusion. "We're not close enough to know what is going on in her home, but her isolation from friends and family is a warning sign."

"Dad and Mom, there is no battering going on in my home," she insisted.

Watching my adult child suffer without doing anything about it had been one of my most painful experiences as a mother.

"Leave adults to sort out their adult problems. What doesn't kill you will make you stronger," my husband philosophized.

"I hope she's not killed in the process of getting stronger."

I wished that Adaugo was still a minor under my roof. I would have taken decisions on her behalf. But my daughter had another allegiance to her husband and her home.

We had long finished dinner that night and were about settling down to sleep when we heard the horn of her car. She came out of the car, rushed into my waiting arms, and broke down in heart-rending sobs. I held my child in my arms and we wept together. Words were unnecessary. Her father was pacing the floor agitatedly. I knew he was holding himself from sobbing too. Society says a crying man is a weak man. But why hold in all the pent up feelings just to appear heroic? Her brothers, impatient young men, were bombarding her with questions.

"Did he beat you?"

"No!" was her emphatic response.

I was relieved. I ran my eyes through her body. No sign of physical assault. Just a battered soul. My sons were swearing how they will kill him for subjecting their sister to torture.

"Where are my granddaughters?" I asked her when the sobbing had subsided.

"He took them from me."

There was no need for further questions.

"Welcome back home, Ada. You're safe here." That was my husband.

She broke down again.

"I failed you, Dad. You brought me up well, but I am a failure. I couldn't make the marriage work. I am a source of shame and embarrassment. I didn't want to bring you reproach and disappointment that you didn't train your daughter well, so I took all the rubbish and stayed, determined to make my marriage work."

"It will still work," my husband told her.

"Dad, will you chase me back to him? I don't want to die." "I will never chase my daughter to her death. We will see how this goes."

We nursed her and humored her and petted her as she regained the peace which she didn't have in her home.

But tradition demands that we ask Chukwudi questions before his family members. So we reached out to the family for discussions. Discussions that proved fruitless.

CHAPTER 3

Obuora's childhood

MY FATHER, NWANKWO, WAS A STEWARD TO REV JOHN LEWARS, A MISSION-
ary with the then Church of Scotland which is now Presbyterian Church
of Nigeria. My mother was a seamstress. He was educated up to Standard
Three level of those days. Just enough for him to be able to understand his
boss's accent. He could speak English and was paid a salary every month.

I remember, with pride, how every December when his boss went for
Christmas break abroad and we visited our village, parents brought letters
written by their sons who had gone to Lagos and other places for Papa to
read and translate for them. They would watch with awe as he looked at the
things scribbled on paper and interpreted the magic to them. I suspected
that he was not always reading those letters correctly because of limitations
in the vocabulary of both himself and the writers because I caught him
once struggling to spell the words. But a one-eyed man is better than the
blind. To cover up for him, once I got to a higher class than he ever attained,
he transferred the job of letter-reading and writing to me. It also filled him
with pride to see his young son reading and interpreting more fluently than
he was ever able to do.

"You see, we always pray for our children to be better than us. They
will be taller, richer, more educated than us," he told his admiring audience.

Living in the mission station exposed me to the strict discipline of
both the missionaries and my father. My father ruled his family with a rod
of iron. We the children and our mother lived in fear of him. Life was orderly and regimented. I grew up having to obey rules of observing hours of

prayer, siesta, not playing football on Sundays, and living life without noise-making. I had to learn to keep a clean environment and personal hygiene.

But little boys were not created to be so mannered and orderly, so my brothers and I were often on a collision course with our disciplinarian dad. We will watch him talk in near whispers to his white boss, bowing and grinning like a cat, but come home and roar at us like a lion. He kept canes of different sizes for each of his four sons. His favorite Bible passage was 'Spare the rod and spoil the child.' The flogging reduced when my eldest brother challenged him with 'Fathers provoke not your children to anger.' But until that day when he was so challenged, we were flogged mercilessly for any and every misdemeanor.

We were flogged for shouting across the fence. We were flogged for playing football during Sir's siesta time. We were flogged for not waking up by ourselves for morning prayers, or for coming late. We were flogged for breaking the globe of the lantern when it was our turn to wash it. We were flogged for urinating on the bed while sleeping. We were flogged for breaking China plates and hiding the ruins. Dad flogged us for covering up for ourselves and for telling lies. The way he was flogging us often made us wonder if he was truly our father. I remember one of my brothers asking our mother to tell us the truth if we were really their children. As an adult and a father, I have come to judge my father more kindly. I now know that he was doing what he considered his best for his family and to retain his job. I heard Mr. Lewars cautioning him to reduce the 'racket' coming from his house. I didn't know the meaning of the word till much later, but Papa made us literarily walk on tiptoes around the house.

Our mother watched helplessly as our father gave his favorite twelve strokes of the cane to culprits. Sometimes, she would plead feebly and un-successfully for mercy. He rehearsed Eli's story to us nearly during every evening prayer. He didn't want God to punish him and us for doing evil.

One day while playing with a pebble, I mistakenly hit the mirror that my father looks at while shaving. As the mirror cracked and fell in pieces, I prayed for death to just take me quietly and quickly, instead of waiting for Papa to kill me in a slow tortuous manner. I contemplated running away, but I didn't know where to run to. Adam hid himself in the garden when he heard the voice of God, so I did the same, hiding in a bush far away from the mission house. My parents called and I didn't answer. Night came and I was still in hiding. I plucked and ate some half-ripe mangoes to satisfy my hunger and thirst. I thought of snakes, but better a snake bite than facing

Papa. I can't tell you what happened. I must have slept off. But I saw his face peering at me in the dark with the hurricane lantern supplying light. I screamed in fear.

I am living proof of the resurrection from the dead because I died and came back. The flogging was such that I couldn't localize the pain. After some time, I wasn't feeling anything again, so I imagined I had died. I saw people in white smiling at me. One big kind-faced being was feeling my forehead. I smiled back. I heard laughter.

"He has regained consciousness. He has come back."

It took a full day for me to regain consciousness and I wasn't in school for one week because of the injuries. The house was gloomy. Mama would look at me and break down in tears. Papa was taciturn. There was no remorse and no apology. Once he entered the house, my brothers and I scampered for safety.

So as a child, I decided that I wasn't going to treat my children so. No child of mine would be flogged. No child would be forced to take a siesta. No child would eat what he doesn't like. No child would sleep except he wants to. Every child would be free to do as they like. I smile as I remember these things because age and experience have made me modify some of these. But my resolve has remained the same: to be the loving father that I didn't have.

The beauty of living in mission quarters is that you start school early. I didn't wait for my right hand to touch my left ear before I followed my two school-age brothers to school. In fact, my mother was relieved because she didn't need to bother about me while babysitting my kid brother and sewing clothes for her customers. One pleasant memory of childhood was falling asleep in the sitting room to the rhythm of my mother's sewing machine.

Mama was loving and caring, and I should have rated her highly but for her insistence on our taking castor oil last Saturday of every month to cleanse our stomach. I think the person who discovered drinking castor oil must have been a sadist! That drink ought to be served to maximum risk criminals as part of their punishment. The taste is horrid!

I started school and it was fun. I could shout and scream with other children as we played football on the pitch, or ran races or played hide and seek. Learning was fun too. The classes reverberated with children's voices chanting times tables.

"Three times three Nine!"

Spelling and dictation. Comparison of adjectives and the laughter and tears that followed the wrong answers.

"Good Gooder Goodest." "Bad Badder Baddest."

The child who got all the answers will have the singular honor and privilege of flogging his classmates who failed the questions.

The short and long breaks! We were each given money to buy snacks, so we bought Puff puff, *moi moi,* and *akara.* We skipped with ropes and played ladders.

The end of the term was the dreaded period, Results were announced in the assembly ground. That was the judgment day. We assembled in trepidation before the Headmaster (representing God) and all the teachers (representing the angels). The instruction was that there should be no noise until he had read out the results from primary one to primary six. You rejoiced in very low tones or mourned in low tones.

After the ordeal in the assembly ground, you carried your result home to your parents who flogged and disgraced you for not coming first.

"Those who took first, do they have two heads?"

I came first in primary one and I noticed I had cracked the code of acceptance and regard from Papa. I saw that the flogging was reducing as I kept doing well in school.

It was normal to write the secondary school entrance examination in primary six, but since I was considered brilliant, Papa instructed me to try from primary five. Even if I didn't do very well, I would have acquired the experience needed to do better. I made a fantastic result, scoring aggregate twenty-eight out of thirty-six. This was the highest result ever scored in the family and I became Papa's favorite son. He took me and my result to his boss who shook my hands warmly and offered to pay for my secondary education. I shook a white man's hand. I wasn't going to forget the experience in a hurry. Papa's eyes brimmed with tears. I had never seen him like that. So he was a normal human being and not a beast of no nation!

I registered in Government College, Afikpo. My motivation was high. I wasn't going to disappoint my white sponsor or my proud father, so I continued working hard. My efforts paid off and I not only made a good result but also secured a scholarship for my university education.

After graduation came the marriage to Nkechi, and with marriage, fatherhood. I loved my daughter dearly, but my love for her couldn't guaranty her happiness in marriage.

CHAPTER 4

Adaugo's family life

I DROPPED IFY AND SOMTO OFF AT THE DAY CARE CENTER. CHUKWUDI and I had jointly taken a decision not to engage another house help. After several hassles to retain one, we decided to register the children at a Day Care. Our experience with Rose was the most disappointing. The girl seemed to be struck with wanderlust, or at least a local variety of it. At a specific time in the day, she would leave the house and visit a nearby building construction site which had a large collection of able-bodied young men whom she claimed were her 'brothers.' I refused to imagine what she must be doing with them.

Things got to a screeching halt when I came home one day to find Somto locked up alone in the house with Rose nowhere in sight. Her tear-stained face showed a child who had cried herself to sleep. Even in her sleep, she was still heaving deeply. The sight tore at my heartstrings.

"Rose! Rose! Rose," I was calling frantically. She came back about an hour later. She had gauged when I would have brought Ify from school.

"Oh, Aunty! You're home already. I went to see that my brother . . . ."

Till tomorrow, I respect myself for the restraint I exercised that day. Inside, I was yearning to give her the beating of her life. But that will violate my principle of not laying hands on a house girl. You see, I am one of those people that take an exception to house girls being vilified. I hate to see other people's children being maltreated simply because the parents are too poor to take care of them.

I thought of all the plans I had for Rose. She seemed to be a bright girl, who if given the opportunity would excel in her studies. She was brought to me in the middle of the term, and I intended that right after her probationary period, I would register her in a nearby secondary school. As she completed her studies and passed with credits I would pay for her undergraduate studies. In later life, she would be grateful to the lady that allowed her to be something useful in life. I could hear my brother's voice in the background of my head.

"My sister, Adaugo, the problem with you is that you are ambitious for people who are not ambitious for themselves." As I sat looking at Rose, I wondered if my brother was right after all. Here I was planning a grand future for a seventeen- year old whose thoughts were focused on the next five hundred naira she would get from her 'brothers.' I had tried counseling. "Do you know that you can get diseases or become pregnant?"

The eyes that met mine showed me she knew about condoms, and what and how exactly they are used. I tried another pitch.

"Life is much more than sleeping with random men and collecting peanuts. You can be a female doctor, engineer or teacher if you control yourself and focus on your studies."

Rose looked at me with pity like one who would say, 'E don tey wey I spoil.' She just couldn't grasp the restraint that an alternative lifestyle could give.

Somebody may blame me for giving up too early, but I did give up. I wasn't going to sacrifice my precious daughter in an effort to recover a girl who had been so sexually abused that she didn't know of an alternative life style.

What if, as she left my eleven month baby at home all alone, the child crawled and touched something or drank something dangerous. The thought sent a chill down my spine.

I counted my losses: my vanity and reputation as Corrector- General and Chief Rescuer of abused women. It wasn't working with Rose.

I took her back to her aunt who brought her to me. She was distraught: "Her father who is my brother is very sick in the village. Her poor mother is coping with five other children. Rose, this woman loves you. They put sugar in your mouth and you spat it out."

Rose didn't apologize. She didn't ask for a second chance. I left her with her aunt and came home.

About a month later, I ran into her aunt on her way to the police station. Another lady had hired Rose as a salesgirl. As usual, she left the shop to quickly visit one of her 'brothers.' Passersby entered the shop and removed some valuables and the madam locked Rose up for theft.

After Rose, we decided on no house girl again and registered Somto in Ify's school.

At the gate to receive her was Aunt Winnie, one cheerful, vivacious teacher that was a great favorite with children and parents.

Somto pattered towards her as I dropped her off. I was smiling to myself. The first few days at the Day Care had been hell. Somto would scream with all her might and main and cling to me. As Aunt Winnie forcefully took her from me and I dashed towards the gate, I would still be hearing her screams. Motherhood is something else. I could distinctly pick out my child's cry even among other crying babies.

I don't know the magic that Aunt Winnie used but after just two weeks, Somto would walk willingly, and at times, joyfully into her waiting arms. That is one woman who enjoys her job. I had already started driving off when the thought came to me. I reversed and honked for Aunt Winnie to come. I wrapped some money into my palms and placed it in hers. "Something for your lunch today, Aunt Winnie." She looked at her hands, mumbled her thanks and I drove off.

I felt a sense of disappointment. I had expected Aunt Winnie to be more effusive with her thanks. Maybe the money I gave her was too small. I was flogging myself. If you want to do good, take your time, and do it well. You acted on the impulse of the moment.

Now see, instead of getting appreciated, you have hurt the psyche of Aunt Winnie by giving her so little that she found it difficult to pretend to be grateful.

For the next week, I was relieved that Aunt Winnie wasn't the teacher on duty to receive the children. For some time, I wouldn't get to see her. I had dropped Somto and zoomed off when I noticed some people were signaling for me to stop. I reversed to the school gate and there was Aunt Winnie.

"I ran out when I saw your car, I want to thank you for the other day. My family didn't have anything on us. That morning, we had just enough money for me to pay for my transport fare to work. As we gathered for morning prayer, we asked God to provide us our daily bread. My husband's business has not been doing well at all, so we are depending on my teacher's salary. I came to work, and you gave me that money. You would notice that I couldn't thank you. I was too surprised for words. So God can answer prayers like this?"

We were both weeping. She continued.

"That day, I thought you were an angel. That money was more than a million naira to me. After school, I rushed to the market and bought garri and vegetables. My husband and children came back home to a hot lunch. They were asking me how manage?"

So much for misunderstanding people. Is it not Shakespeare that said, 'There's no art to find the mind's construction on the face?' If there's any skill I would like to learn, it is mind-reading: how to understand the unspoken intentions of people.

I left Aunt Winnie and drove off.

How I wish I was this wrong concerning my husband, Chukwudi. I have this niggling discomfort when I think of our relationship. Is there a gulf growing between us, or am I the one imagining that there is?

CHAPTER 5

Chukwudi's traditional marriage

I MET ADAUGO WHEN I WAS A TWENTY-THREE YEAR OLD UNDERGRADUATE in Electrical Engineering. She was just seventeen and in secondary school. My friends teased me for being a cradle-snatcher but I believe a man should be much older than his woman. I had many years to go before settling down. That would give her ample time to grow and mature.

"Catch them young," my friend, Alex, teased me.

I can't recall which of my friends told us about Adaugo. He just mentioned one very brilliant and beautiful girl who can be nurtured into a wife material and Alex and I decided to check her out. Finding a woman with brain and beauty combined was getting rare. The girls I had tried to date only talked of wigs and cosmetics. No intelligent discussions. No life plan.

I had my fair share of trying to date girls. Alex who was more worldly-wise had taught me how to compose love texts and to shoot my shot. I professed undying love to girls I felt absolutely nothing for. I wanted desperately to belong and to share juicy stories too. But deep down, I knew what I really wanted: a committed relationship that would lead to marriage. Adaugo was in the boarding house, so how to meet her was not going to be easy. Alex and I did our due diligence. We got to know their visiting day. What would we tell her we came to do?

On one of her visiting days, we arrived at the school towards evening. That way, we won't meet her parents as they would have gone. We sent a girl to call her and waited.

In no time, two slim, very pretty girls walked towards us. This was not what I expected. She had brought a friend for moral support. How do I know which one is Adaugo since I had never met her? My head was reeling with confusion.

I am forever grateful to a junior student who passed by and greeted "Good evening, Senior Adaugo."

One of those beauties responded with her own "Good evening."

I inwardly did the sign of the cross in appreciation.

Adaugo was the prettier girl. For some seconds, I just stared stupidly at them and couldn't say anything. Blame it on my inexperience but I was startled by her presence. Come on say something. Don't be a moron.

"Hello, Adaugo. My name is Alex. Meet my friend, Chukwudi."

This is bad. Alex is already preparing to snatch this girl from me.

"Hello, Alex and Chukwudi," she replied sweetly. "My friend is Nma. I begged her to accompany me because I heard that visitors were looking for me."

"Adaugo," I began, "I'm your cousin's close friend. I am Eugene's friend." It worked. She smiled. At me.

"We're in the same university."

I thank God I remembered that one.

"We were just passing by (that's not true but all is fair in love and war) and decided to say 'hello.' At least I can tell him I saw his very beautiful cousin."

A wider smile from her. It was working. Family ties and a strong compliment. Women never get tired of hearing how beautiful they are.

"Thank you so much for stopping by," Adaugo said.

Good command of English spoken in a frank unassuming manner.

We chatted more with both girls. Nma was as engaging as her friend but was also careful not to take all the attention from her.

We found out that they were both Art students. They enjoy reading novels and were members of the Young Writer's Club and active members of the Christian fellowship in school. They were obviously God-fearing girls, which explains why they came together so that they would hold each other accountable. All these confirmed one thing: wife materials, one thousand yards long.

As we left them forty-five minutes later, I did not doubt that my search for a wife was over.

"I will marry that girl," I told Alex.

"You can't be so forward," Alex argued. "I got to know about her before you did, so I would try to get her interested in me first. You're not the only one that likes good things."

Alex and I were fighting over Adaugo.

We argued all the way back to school. I was pleading with him to leave Adaugo for me.

At last, he was persuaded. He told me he could see that I had fallen in love at first sight. He also recalled how easily Adaugo had conversed with me. So convincing her to date me will be easy. I was happy I had my friend by my side, and we will plot how to secure the love of this intelligent, beautiful, and Godly girl.

Alex said something that surprised me. "I actually like Nma too. She's not as drop-dead gorgeous as your Adaugo, but she's pretty and wise. I wouldn't mind marrying her."

We were excited like little boys who had just been given new toys. I was happy for him and he was happy for me. We were planning our future: two friends who will marry two ladies that are friends. Endless family visits, children who will grow up relating like siblings. We will be each other's best man and our wives will be each other's chief bridesmaids.

This was the pre-mobile phone era, so communication was by letters. Without wasting time, I wrote to Adaugo. I told her that her cousin was fine. I actually went looking for him and hinted that I just happened to pass by his cousin's school and stopped to greet her. I could see suspicion on his face, but I didn't pursue it further. Let him do his worst. He won't marry his cousin. I will.

Eugene was a likable Civil Engineering student. I had met him when we took general engineering courses together. I think my excitement in talking about Adaugo must have been obvious. He came to my class to look for me some days later. I was surprised.

"Please, promise me that you won't take advantage of Adaugo's naivety and age," he pleaded.

"I promise you even more than that. Adaugo is not the average 'bush-meat'. My intentions are honorable. If God supports us, I would love to marry her."

"Promise you won't touch her till then," he insisted.

"I will. But I want you not to divulge my secret to your family until we're ready."

He promised me that if he doesn't see any degeneration in her conduct or result, then he won't raise any alarm. We became friends after that.

In the letter, I thanked her for making out time to talk with us. I ended the letter with "Take care of your beautiful self for me" and a love sign.

She's so young. Just seventeen but I hope she gets the hint. She replied! She actually did. Once I saw the name on the letter, I was too excited to read the contents. I hid it in my lecture bag and let my imaginations run wild. It was difficult to listen to the lecturer. He might well be talking to himself. My thoughts were engaged: Adaugo replied to my letter. That was enough green light. The letter was short and didn't betray any emotions, but the fact that she replied was enough encouragement.

I followed up with more letters and periodic visits. At first, she was skeptical of my attention. She made it obvious to me that her studies mattered a lot more to her than boys. I didn't bug her with professions of love; there will be time for that later. Instead, I bought her JAMB past questions and model answers. I bought her 'serious' novels, not Mills and Boon or Harlequin series, which had nauseating pornographic content. I bought her Buchi Emecheta's *The Bride Price* and Alex Haley's *Roots*. She had told me that she wanted to be a lawyer and I loved her ambition.

My love for Adaugo was of a pure, unselfish kind. I was going to groom this beautiful and brilliant girl to be a wonderful, financially independent, and responsible wife. I saw her vividly in my future; a great future with our lovely children, boys and girls, surrounding our table. I saw that she loved me too. It wasn't the love of a starry-eyed teenage girl, but in a manner that was surprising for her age. I saw loyalty and purpose.

By the long vacation, as I would learn later, her parents had noticed. Certain things had given her away. Her Mom, bless her soul, had suspected that her daughter was getting emotionally attached to somebody. She smiled more than usual and had a faint glint around her eyes. She used the opportunity when Adaugo stepped out of the house to go through her stuff and that was when she saw one of my love letters. All hell was let loose. Her father was alerted to the impending doom which such a relationship will attract.

"You'll get pregnant and drop out of school."

"You are still too small to get involved with a boy! "Your grades will suffer"

"You will not amount to anything if you continue like this" "You are a prostitute already."

It was all too much that she broke down in tears. "Promise us that you'll call off the relationship immediately," her father said,

"I promise you, Dad," she answered tearfully.

"Okay, should we withdraw you from school so that you can go and marry Chukwudi now?" her mother queried.

"No, Mom. I like to go to school. I am not ready for marriage."

Her brother brought a piece of paper and she wrote the letter which was sent to me.

Dear Chukwudi,

I am very sorry that we can't remain friends. I am too young to be keeping such a relationship. Don't write to me again.

Don't come to visit me again.

Bye Adaugo

My hands shook as I read the letter. Then I wept. I was heartbroken. This is injustice. I hadn't taken advantage of her youth. All my hopes for our future came crashing down. How will I find a girl like Adaugo again? No wonder Romeo died with Juliet! I felt like committing suicide. What was the value of being alive if I couldn't spend it with the person that I love? What future could I look forward to if it was a loveless future? I didn't attend lectures for a whole week. I was also not eating well. Adaugo was my life. How could she just end the relationship like that? I would have rushed to her school to demand an explanation, but she had said I shouldn't even visit her. I wanted her to tell me her reasons. I could sense that it wasn't another man in her life. I know that she's just seventeen, but is it a crime to love somebody at that age? Didn't our mothers fall in love and marry at sixteen? I didn't even ask her to drop out of school and marry me immediately. I just wanted her to love me and be there for me in the future. What was wrong with that?

When I couldn't bear the torture any longer, I confided in Alex. I showed him the letter which was the cause of my misery, but he saw a silver lining there which I hadn't noticed.

"See, she didn't say that she hates you. She only said that she is still young which is true. She can still marry you when she has grown older," he comforted me.

I thought about Alex's perspective. He may be right. In fact, he is right. Will I be happy if my seventeen-year-old daughter starts seeing a man?

Won't I be worried about her? It is true that I had never as much as kissed her but which responsible parent would not be suspicious of that type of association? Something told me that her family must have put pressure on her because we didn't quarrel or have a misunderstanding, so there was no excuse or other explanation for the letter.

Alex who had also been pursuing his friendship with Nma with similar vigor slowed down, He said he was learning from my experience. We agreed to keep our eyes on the two girls from afar while working on ourselves so that we will deserve their hands in marriage in the future.

I picked up my spirits. Instead of drifting into another relationship, I decided to focus on my studies, graduate with a good grade, secure a job, and then formally and respectfully ask for her hand in marriage. No reasonable parent will antagonize a hard-working and ambitious young man.

Wait for me, Adaugo! No, don't wait. Grow up for me. With time, our dreams will mature to reality.

My resolve paid off. I graduated with a Second Class Honors Upper Division, completed the compulsory national service, secured a job with Volt Engineering, and got a modest one-bedroom apartment. Everything was working according to plan.

Without necessarily intruding, I had kept my eyes on Adaugo from afar. She had completed her secondary education and entered the university. She didn't secure admission for Law but English studies. Still okay by me. Was I really keen on an argumentative *over-sabi* wife?

I didn't need anybody's approval to visit her. I went in search of her at her university.

I knew every detail including her room number so I just went to Eyoita Hall and asked them to call me Adaugo from Room 309.

She screamed when she saw who her visitor was.

At first, I couldn't tell if it was surprise or delight or both.

But it was obvious that she was happy to see me.

I noticed that the university had not changed her in any negative way. She was decently dressed, spoke about her studies, and had joined a campus fellowship.

"Can we do lunch?" I asked hesitantly. Her eyes shot up with caution. "Nothing more than lunch, I promise."

She agreed and I took her to a nearby eatery outside the campus.

She asked about my job and I told her all there was to tell. Then she said something that surprised me.

"I want to thank you, Chukwudi, for showing interest in me in my secondary school days. My family was worried but I still believe that God brought you as a friend into my life. It was difficult convincing my parents that the relationship was in all purity. You helped me focus on my studies. You also treated me with respect. Somehow relating with you kept me off other unserious relationships with boys because I was always comparing them with you and they were always falling short." I had heard all that I needed to hear. She still loved me and she was not engaged to any man. I resumed our relationship by occasional visits and letters.

It was time to formally let her know my intentions. I didn't have much money, but I bought a simple ring, invited her for lunch and at the restaurant, I went down on one knee.

"I have loved you since I met you. Through the years that we were not communicating, I still loved you and was working hard to improve myself to deserve you. I don't have all the money to guarantee us an easy life but if you are ready to start humbly with me, we can help each other and grow the kingdom of our dream. Will you marry me, Adaugo?"

She was weeping as she said a faint "Yes."

I slipped the ring on her finger and we hugged.

Other diners at the eatery had paused from their chattering and eating. The whole restaurant went quiet as they watched the proceedings. When she said 'yes,' there was an eruption of joy. Total strangers were clapping and cheering. Some were wiping tears from their eyes.

I was so happy!

Adaugo informed her parents. They raised their objections: I was a young graduate. My mother was a poor widow. I was the oldest child and will have a huge responsibility. Was she ready to start so low? I didn't have a car yet and life will be tough. But Adaugo stood by me and by her decision.

She loved me and we will start small. She was now an adult and she knew what she wanted for her life. They gave us their consent and blessing.

I announced our engagement to my mother and her reactions was predictable. I didn't blame her one bit.

I was the oldest of eight children and the first graduate among them. She expected that having secured a job, I will face the sponsoring of my siblings' education, all seven of them. And here I was talking about falling in love and wanting to marry a wife. If I followed her plans, at what age will I finish raising seven siblings before planning for my own family?

I intended to help as much as I could but I wasn't going to wholly sacrifice my happiness and future solving other people's problems.

"Mama listen. Adaugo is a very humble girl. You're getting a daughter. Marrying her will not stop me from helping you and my younger ones. It will even help me not to waste money on girlfriends or relationships that will not lead anywhere."

My mother knows just how much pressure she can put on me and when to stop. Not being educated herself, she thinks of me as being the smartest, greatest, highest genius she has ever seen.

"No problem, son. God will be with you. If your wife comes and she hates me, well . . ." she broke down in tears.

"Why will she hate you? She loves me and will love you too."

I told Adaugo that I wanted her to love and respect my mother.

"Why is she worried? I will love her for your sake," she reassured me.

On a Saturday when I was free from work, I went with her from Rumuimo where I was working to Okiti to see my mother. On the way, I was worried about many things. I wished that I had bought a car first. Adaugo's father had a car. Was I right to be dragging this obviously privileged girl down to my level? Did she genuinely love me or she was pitying me and managing me?

"A penny for your thoughts," she teased me. She wanted to know why my face was creased.

"Ada, are you sure this is what you want to do? Will you follow through on your decision? Is youthful exuberance not the driving force? Won't you have preferred a more financially comfortable man?" All my vulnerabilities and insecurities kept pouring out.

She dovetailed her fingers in mine and answered " I know who I want to spend forever with. He holds my hand right now."

Other passengers on the fourteen-sitter bus tried to avoid looking at us, but we could see them smiling at us. I promised myself that a car will be a priority right after the marriage rites. I wasn't going to subject her to this uncomfortable trip anymore.

I was worried too about how my mother will receive her. You could never tell with mothers. A friend took a girl home to show his mother, and without any explanation, the mother rejected the girl. She claimed her maternal instincts told her the girl spelled like bad news. The man was hurt, but he later discovered so many details about the lady's past that would have prevented him from marrying her. Will Mama 'sense' any danger with

Adaugo? What will I do if Mama claims that she saw Adaugo as a witch in her dreams? I knew that I will still go ahead with the marriage, but it will strain our relationship, maybe for life. Women are usually sensitive about the first reception from their in-laws.

I asked Adaugo's opinion "Will you still marry me if my mother dislikes you at first sight?"

"Never. You will go with the wind," she shocked me.

"But I thought you love me very much."

"I love you very much that I won't like to come between you and your Mom. It will be selfish of me and unfair to you to impose myself on your family if they don't want me. Leaving you will actually be an act of love. You can marry another girl, but your family remains your family."

Her line of argument didn't make sense, but I let her be. I thought the more romantic answer should have been that she would stick to me as we fight for what we both shared. If I knew that was how she thought, I would have gone ahead of her to beg Mama. But now it was late.

We arrived Okiti and the dreaded introduction took place. Mama let out a shout of joy when she saw us. She was delighted.

"Everybody come and see my new daughter. She's so pretty. I knew my son will marry a lovely wife."

I was happy and Adaugo was happy that she was accepted.

So much for my worries.

"My daughter, don't sit like a visitor. Go to the kitchen and serve yourself and your husband's food."

That was my mother's height of informality and acceptance—to allow anyone to put a hand in her soup pot. Even we her children didn't have such a privilege.

"I have been praying that Chukwudi will not marry a wife but will bring to me a daughter. You are the daughter not wife. You will be the second mother to these children. God will give you your own sons and daughters."

"Thanks, Mama for accepting me. I promise you that I won't take your son from you. We shall be one big happy family."

I took her to visit Uncle Nwagbo. He liked her instantly. His wife promised to introduce Adaugo to the association of wives of the family. She showed her the uniforms that they wore for weddings or burials. His children clung to her and were crying when we were ready to go.

"You see how my children love you," Uncle Nwagbo teased her. "They can sense that you will bring their brothers and sisters. Very soon, you will see wonders. I trust my son, Chukwudi." He ended with a wink.

She accepted foodstuffs from Uncle Nwagbo and my mother. We returned to Rumuimo.

I saved up for the marriage rites. When I felt ready, I was formally introduced to Adaugo's family as a suitor.

Her parents are well educated and had jobs. Very different family settings. They seemed to like me too.

"Chukwudi, my daughter has told us a lot about you," that was Adaugo's father. "We can see that you are a responsible and hardworking young man." I thanked him profusely. From then on, I became an accepted and frequent visitor to the family. I warmed up to her siblings. I could detect uneasiness on her brothers' part but I put it down to rivalry. We agreed on a date for the 'knocking at the door' ceremony.

I came with my mother and Uncle Nwagbo to meet Adaugo's father, mother, one uncle and one aunt. I could see that my mother was awed by the seeming opulence of Adaugo's family. She had never associated with senior-level civil servants before. My marriage was an upward movement on the social ladder for her too. She sat timidly and uncomfortably on the well-padded settee and left my uncle to lead in the discussions. The living room, though not ostensibly opulent, was tastefully furnished to befit their social status. On the wall were her parents' wedding pictures, as well as pictures of all their four children at different stages of growth: all the others, but Adaugo, had pictures to mark their sixth month, first birthday, and sixth birthday when they started primary school. Adaugo's earliest picture was after her third birthday which coincided with the end of the Civil War. They even had a dining area with a table and six chairs. The photos were lined according to their order of birth. So it was a gallery of the family's history. Unlike my home that had a long hard seat without pads. There was no dining area. Food, like rice, was served in a large tray and as we gathered to struggle for the often insufficient meals, it was the survival of the fittest. Mama had to suspend her eating to settle internecine wars arising from trying to pin down who exactly among us stole the pieces of meat without waiting for it to be equitably shared.

My eyes went to the lovely floral curtains on the windows unlike ours that Mama covered with old wrappers that she was no longer using. The dining table was set with delicious- looking foods and drinks, tall glasses, and chinaware. There was cutlery neatly arranged. I swallowed hard. I have to work hard to provide Adaugo with this level of comfort that she was already used to.

I saw Mama shivering. I begged my parents-in-law for permission to turn off the air-conditioners. They understood immediately and apologized to Mama. She only smiled back and called herself a village woman.

We presented them with the traditional bottle of wine and my uncle formally told them of my intention to marry their daughter and of my family's support for the marriage. They called Adaugo and she confirmed that she loves me and will marry me. That was all that needed to be done and refreshments followed. I knew Mama wasn't going to use the forks and knives, so I told my in-laws to provide us with water in a wash hand basin. She ate as carefully and shyly as if she was the new wife that we came to marry. We collected the list for the traditional marriage and agreed on a future date for the full rites to be concluded.

Once we were out of their house and left to ourselves, Mama's fears came tumbling out. "Why did you choose a girl from a rich family? How shall we satisfy them? How will she be submissive to you when her parents are living like kings? A poor boy like you deserves to marry a lowly girl so that they can start a life together."

Fortunately for me, Uncle Nwagbo was there.

"Nne, It's better he marries from a rich family. She won't come with family responsibility so that together, they can face his own. If you add poverty to poverty, you will get greater poverty. Let us relate to those who are higher than us. They can lift us. They can even help to get jobs for your other children once they finish school. Adaugo has parents who are living peacefully together. She will make a good wife like her mother."

I didn't know how to thank Uncle Nwagbo enough. Mama was satisfied and the rest of our discussions centered on the size of meat she was given and how regal their house was.

Discussing the marriage arrangements nearly caused friction with Adaugo's parents. They wanted a fairly elaborate wedding, but knowing the responsibilities to my family, I put my foot down: I wanted a traditional marriage after which Adaugo and I will go and quietly wed in court. Her parents were adamant. There must be an elaborate wedding and they will help me to fund it, but I didn't want to start my marriage on such a footing. Adaugo stood by me, and I was so proud of her. We settled on 'Gage and Go' alias traditional marriage only.

Even for the traditional marriage, I insisted on coming with only ten members of my family. I pleaded with my in-laws not to invite the whole village. I wanted a simple ceremony with minimal cost. I had heard tales of bridegrooms who borrowed to finance their weddings and started their marriages with heavy debts that broke the homes. They had hoped to get enough financial gifts from friends and relatives to offset the loans, but were disappointed. I wasn't going to rob a bank to marry.

I was relieved to see only about twenty people in her father's compound when we arrived. There was a single canopy that could seat fifty people in front of their house. Music was supplied from the stereo set which they moved from the living room to the front of the house. A cameraman was on hand to cover both photography and videography. There was no elaborate decoration and no cake. Budget marriage! I wasn't going to borrow money to impress people who didn't know I existed just to make a point that I could afford a lavish wedding. It would also be wrong for Ada's parents to give me a fantastic girl and run the expenses for marrying her off too. Everything was on course.

After the customary greetings and presentation of kola nut, my ever-dependable uncle, Nwagbo, who was our spokesperson informed the house of our mission. It's amazing that even though they say the same things at every marriage, it still sounds interesting. Especially if you're the person involved.

"One of our sons said he found a beautiful flower in your compound," Uncle Nwagbo began. "The flower is very beautiful, but lovely as it is, it won't be of any use to you if you keep it. So we have come to ask you for permission to take that beautiful flower."

He dropped the bottle of wine on the table. Adaugo's uncle responded.

"We have so many flowers, all of them very beautiful and we don't know the one you're asking for. So we will ask them to come out. Just point at the one you want."

Then followed a parade. Girls of nubile age came out one after the other. As they came out we shout "No! Not this one." After five girls, Adaugo came out dressed in George fabric with ornamental beads on her waist, neck and head, and carrying a feathery white horsetail. She danced gently into the open space between the canopy and the house. My mouth dropped. I had never seen her looking so gorgeous. Our photographer must have imagined himself as doing paparazzi. The camera was clicking and blinking nonstop.

"Yaaa. That's the one."

We all shouted and clapped in unison. My clan members rose and sprayed currency notes on her.

"Adaugo my daughter," her father addressed her. "These men have come for you. They say they want your hand in marriage. See the things they brought. The yams, the drinks, other gifts, and fabrics. When we give our daughters out in marriage they remain married. They never come back. If we accept these things, you are married and you must remain married. Please, tell us here what we should do. Should we accept them and their gifts or send them away."

We all hold our breaths.

"Daddy, please accept their gifts," said Adaugo. More clapping and she left.

The elders from both sides retire to a room to negotiate the bride price. I accompany them but I am not allowed to talk.

Adaugo's father brings a pack of broomsticks, clears his throat, and begins.

"We don't sell our daughters. What we are doing is a mere traditional formality because the marriage starts when young people agree to marry. We also don't force our in-laws to pay more than what they can afford. We don't fleece them. So here are some broomsticks. Each is the equivalent of one hundred thousand naira only. You know our daughter. You also know how deep your pocket is. Now pick the number of broomsticks that represent the amount you can pay."

My uncle started picking. My heart jumped when he picked ten. One million naira! Where am I going to get such a huge sum to pay as bride price?

We were all watching him.

"Our in-law, because you're already our in-law, I picked ten broomsticks worth a million naira because that is what we are ready to pay. Your wonderful daughter is worth even more than that. But we are not paying all that amount today. Nobody ever completes paying for a wife in a day because she's not an article of trade. So we are going to drop a token of ten thousand naira."

I released the air I was holding.

He counted the money and dropped it on the tray. Adaugo's father got up.

"My in-laws, I thank you. I appreciate your gesture. I love my daughter, but I can't marry her. I told you that we are not selling her. I want to return the money to you. All I'm begging you is to take good care of my child."

"Your child is in good hands," my uncle comes in again. "All our men are fertile. The groom today has seven other siblings, so nine months from now, you will see wonders."

Everybody burst out laughing.

"Twins, triplets. It's your daughter that will be running from pregnancy."

They sent a token of two thousand naira to Adaugo's mother. I was wondering what exactly she will do with such a paltry sum, but it was the culture.

We returned to the small canopy where guests were seated. Adaugo was sent for again. She came out tying the double wrapper, blouse, and head tie of a married woman. I was wearing the same material with her. She knelt respectfully before her father.

"Adaugo, your husband's family has fulfilled all the rites to make you their wife. But there are so many handsome young men here that I don't know which of them is doing all these things for us. Take this glass of wine from me, go and look for that your husband. When you find him bring him here and let me bless both of you."

Adaugo collected the drink. I knew she had seen where I was, but she was doing a pretend search. All the men were begging her for her drink but she wouldn't give them.

"No, you're not the one. He's finer than you." This got everybody laughing.

Eventually, she approached my seat. I was grinning from ear to ear. She knelt in front of me and offered me a glass of wine. I drank it all up and stuck some money in the cup by way of appreciation.

I got up and helped her rise up from the ground.

We marched to where her parents were seated and knelt respectfully before them. It was time for their blessings. For several seconds her father couldn't talk. I looked up to see tears rolling down his cheeks. It was an emotional moment. Adaugo was crying too.

"My daughter is such a sweet girl. If a father could marry his daughter, today's ceremony would have been unnecessary because I would have married Adaugo. Take care of her. Don't let me regret this decision. God will bless you two with wealth and sound health. Go, my daughter. I am waiting to carry and bless my grandchildren."

The prayer of blessing was over. As we stood up to go to the bridal seats arranged for us, my father-in-law stopped us abruptly.

"Adaugo, show us a secret. Touch the part of Chukwudi's body that attracted him to you."

Without hesitation, she touched my nose. More laughter, food, drinks, and dancing and it was time to take my bride home.

Among their gifts to their daughter, they made a strange presentation to my family. Her father brought saplings of coconut and kolanut trees and asked that they be planted in my family house in his daughter's honor.

"Your marriage will be like these trees in procreation, longevity, wealth, and joy."

Adaugo and I would discuss on end which of us is which of the trees. We settled on me being the kolanut while she is the coconut tree.

My father-in-law suggested a court wedding and I agreed with him. We will do that later. The traditional marriage was the most valid of the marriages. Secondly, we were not planning to travel out of the country where we will need a marriage certificate for the processing of visas, so there was no hurry. We settled down and life was sweet and nice. Till I met Amaka.

CHAPTER 6

Adaugo's vulnerabilities

TRUE TO MY PARENTS' BLESSINGS, I GOT PREGNANT LESS THAN THREE
months after we got married. Chukwudi was overjoyed.

"Now I know that l am a real man. He's a boy and we shall have so
much father and son time together."

Nine months later, I gave birth to a girl. I thought my husband would
be disappointed but he was visibly delighted with our pretty little daughter.

"We shall call her Ifunanya. Love. Because I love you and I love her a
lot."

We took turns changing her diapers. She was the joy of our lives and
the apple of our eyes. We doted on her.

Eighteen months later, our second daughter arrived. I noticed that
Chukwudi was not as excited as before. He told me he was relieved that I
survived pregnancy and delivery. His attitude rubbed off on me. Somehow,
I felt insufficient. As if it was my fault that I had a second daughter. Maybe
if I had tried hard or done some things differently I could have had a son.
Someone quipped that women are the gatekeepers of patriarchy. I was fresh
out of labor and instead of celebrating my adorable daughter, tears of disappointment were falling from my eyes. I had failed once again to give my
husband the son he desired. What if the next and the next and the next
pregnancies produced nothing else but female babies?

My mother scolded me out of this nasty mood. She was pissed off
with me that in this day and age with so many positive female role models,
I was still thinking like an old-fashioned wife who felt that giving birth to

sons validated her existence. She reminded me that it was Chukwudi whose chromosomes determined the sex of our babies. She reasoned with me that girl children took better care of their parents in old age than boy children. One of her younger brothers had decided against having more children after he had two daughters. He told his family that he had asked God to bless him with two daughters and no sons. He was going to invest all his time, love, and money on his girls and make them enviable points of reference in the future. She accused me of ingratitude, because, while many women of my age were longing for a child to love and hold, I was griping that I didn't get the sex I wanted. What if I had died in delivery? My husband would have replaced me with another woman within the shortest possible time and his life will go on. Or the baby had died? If my husband didn't want my daughter, she wanted her granddaughter.

That settled it for me. I poured out my love in Somto. There was to be no preferential treatment. She must not sense, later in life, that I was anything but delighted and privileged to have her. I advised my husband to do the same. He needed it because he was already treating Ifunanya as his favorite child.

Somto's birth seemed to bring us good fortune. He received a double promotion in his place of work and was finally able to get me a small car. He had bought one for himself shortly before the arrival of our first daughter. When my due date was approaching during the first pregnancy, he was scared that I might fall into labor either late in the night or the early hours of the morning when it will be difficult to find a car to transport me to the hospital for delivery.

We saved up and bought a car. I smile when I remember the pride on his face as he drove his wife and daughter home from the hospital. His mother was beaming with smiles too. She had a son who was a car owner. My parents were proud of us. They were glad that I had such a responsible husband. They didn't need much financial assistance from us, but we presented them with occasional gifts especially during festivities. He was helping his siblings by paying for them to get an education too. I was contributing whatever I could from the little money I was making as a receptionist in a private law firm. But the bulk of our bills was picked by my husband.

We moved from the one-bedroom apartment to a more spacious two-bedroom flat. We bought a piece of land and began building our own house. We had decided that we would move from the two-bedroom flat to our building and everything was on course. We celebrated our fifth anniversary by moving into our house. Our families on both sides celebrated with us. They had gathered for the house warming party. My husband told Alex his friend:

"When I hear the word 'landlord', I wonder what that means. Who are they? What do they look like?"

"Just thank your stars that you have a good wife," Alex would remind him. "If she was wasteful and extravagant, you won't be where you are."

"That our trip to your secondary school was the best investment I have ever made of time and money. The dividends are awesome. If given another chance, I would make the same trip over and over again." He teased me.

Alex was there with Nma and their two children. They had a boy and a girl. Even though I loved my two daughters, I sometimes felt envious of their balanced family. I will soon get pregnant, and I hoped it will be a boy. I had learned about sex selection through timed intercourse and I was going to use it to achieve my desire.

But I wasn't getting pregnant as soon as I would have liked. Somto was nearly three and I was yet to get pregnant. Chukwudi told me he wasn't bothered. But I was.

When I mentioned it to Nma, she accused me of ingratitude. "You already have two bubbly daughters to love. What of those who don't have one. Some are praying to get pregnant even if they miscarry or have a stillbirth."

I don't blame her. I didn't expect her to understand. She had both sexes as children and looked like she was already pregnant for the third. It wouldn't matter to her whether it was a boy or girl since she had both. This third one was just to complete their family, she had confided in me. I was happy for her, but there was a tinge of envy.

How come some people could just get pregnant when they want and others couldn't, even after previous pregnancies? I discovered that the pain of not getting pregnant at will is nearly the same as when you've never been pregnant. I remembered others who had only a child. What if I never had more children? I was yearning for a son. Ify and Somto were asking me to give them a little brother. I was vulnerable and insecure. What if I failed to give my husband a son? Will he be satisfied with our daughters or will he marry someone who will give him boys? We didn't wed in the church. Will he have enough commitment to stick to me?

A second cause of worry was my job. Since I graduated, I had not secured well-paying employment. I had been moving from one organization to the other, receiving peanuts as salary. If my marriage crashed because of the absence of a son, how will I survive financially with my daughters? As it was, I was wholly at my husband's mercy financially. It wasn't pleasant. I tried to silence my fears, but the more I tried, the more they were taking root. I shared some of my anxieties with my husband and his response was always the same: "You worry yourself too much. We have two gorgeous daughters. You will get pregnant again in God's own time." But what if I had another daughter as a third child? Or couldn't get pregnant again? Won't he feel too disappointed?

I had heard of men who abandoned their wives in the hospital to pay their delivery fees. Their offense was that they had the audacity to give birth to a third or fourth baby girl. If they had tried hard enough, they would have had a boy, but they stubbornly chose to have yet another girl. The insensitive men were university graduates who had learned about the chromosomes and how it was the husband that determined the sex of the baby.

I couldn't share all my secret fears with Chukwudi. He would think I was crazy if I asked him if he would marry another wife if I failed to give him a son.

His mother wasn't helping matters either. All her prayers for me centered on the coming grandson:"Don't worry, my daughter. God will bless you with a son in your next pregnancy." So my two daughters didn't count as grandchildren yet. "These girls will be married off. But you will have the boy who will stay," she reasoned.

But do the boys really stay? Was her son staying with her? Has he not moved as I also moved from my parent's home?

She wasn't the only one wishing me a boy. Friends and family joined in the chant.

"When the boy comes, you will know you have children in the house. These your daughters are so neat and orderly. You won't know what we go through." That was from Nma, my friend. She made it seem like there was a special club with secrets which only they who have the privilege of having sons belonged. This emphasized my inadequacy.

"Your girls are not heavy eaters. When their brother comes, you will experience what it means to have a healthy eater. This my son can finish a giant bowl of cereal in two seconds." That was the wisdom a mother shared with me in church while we were feeding our children. I nodded in admiration. I had nothing to counter her, so she continued.

"Right from pregnancy, it feels different. I think that this rascal was doing gymnastics in my womb. He was literally kicking my husband out of the bed! The labor was different too. You know if it's a girl, she would take her time to wear a fine dress, look for matching shoes and leisurely apply make- up before she comes out to show herself to the world. They do that right from the womb. But boys don't have any time to waste. This scoundrel was born in a taxi. He couldn't wait for us to get to the hospital."

I could only laugh, admire and wish I had similar experiences to share. The women made it seem like until you have given birth to a boy, you have never really been pregnant. People imagine that it's men that put pressure on the women, but it was fellow women who emphasized my incompleteness for not having a son just yet.

Was I right or was I imagining that my husband was getting distant from me? He seemed a bit more irritable. He answered my questions in a gruff manner and complained of being too busy and tired to attend to family commitments. I saw the gradual changes and I could only hope for the best and pray that it's not going to be as bad as I think.

CHAPTER 7

Chukwudi receives Amaka at home

I MET AMAKA AT ALEX'S CHILD DEDICATION PARTY. I HAD GONE WITH MY family, but after the food and drinks, Adaugo went home with the girls. I stayed back with the 'boys' watching an Arsenal versus Manchester United match. Amaka came later with a contact of Alex's.

As she walked in, our eyes met and she smiled. I felt a warm sensation in my stomach. I smiled back, looking foolish.

My instinct suddenly rose on red alert. This curvaceous smiling woman was a threat. I remembered a discussion I had with Alex. I had tried to convince him that I loved Adaugo so much that it was impossible for me to be attracted to someone else. But he had argued that being in love didn't guarantee not falling in love with someone else. That with time, you may meet someone more beautiful or handsome, more intelligent, or romantic than your partner. The commitment you made to stay in the relationship would carry you through those moments. Then you would stay faithful, not because of the absence of temptation, but because of your choice and the value you placed on your body and your family.

This discussion had taken place when I noticed that Alex was having an affair. He called it an innocent fling, but I couldn't say the same about the relationship. I felt for Nma who is my wife's closest friend. I was wondering what he saw in that lady who didn't hold a candle to his wife. A few months later, he was tired of the lady and returned body and soul to Nma. She hadn't even noticed, so there was obviously no harm done.

All these talks appeared like a fairy tale until I met Amaka.

Her contact introduced her to us and after the usual friendly banter, they settled for their refreshments.

As she was leaving, she asked me for my phone number. I was taken aback. So girls now hit on men in such a bold manner? She read my expression.

"I just want your number so that you can assist some of us with a job search. I heard you work with Volt, so you can help us secure jobs or IT placement," she explained.

It would have been rude if I didn't oblige, so I gave her my phone number.

The vain part of me also felt good that I was still handsome enough for girls to be making such direct overtures to me.

I tried to push all thoughts of her out of my mind. I didn't even bother to save her number.

When my phone rang during my lunch break on Monday, I couldn't tell who was calling. It was Amaka. She asked after my job and family. She said she was just calling to maintain contact until she will need my help.

Without fully considering the implications, I invited her for lunch, and she readily agreed. We met at the agreed eatery and that was the beginning of my fascination with Amaka.

She wasn't as pretty as Adaugo by any stretch of the imagination, but she was lively. In fact, she was everything my wife was not. Adaugo was tall and stately, but Amaka had more flesh and full rounded hips. Where Adaugo was modest and restrained, she was bold and loquacious. She was oozing sensuality and acted like she didn't have a care in the world. I hadn't laughed so hard and so long as I did in the one hour we spent chattering during my lunch break.

Without meaning to, I had told her details of my family life.

"How many children?" she asked.

"Two daughters. Lovely sons on the way."

"It doesn't matter," she said.

It struck me. What didn't matter? My having only daughters at the time? What did Amaka mean? Before I could probe her further, she had changed the topic. There was no dull moment. That lunch date was followed by other ones. There were also numerous phone calls and chats. I had to tell myself the truth. I cared about Amaka a whole lot. I remembered her birthday and bought gifts for her. When she told me she had accommodation problem, I advanced her the money.

Adaugo, I could tell, was sensing that all was not well between us, but I justified it with the thought that I wasn't committing adultery; just being a big uncle and 'mentor' to a young lady.

Alex warned me that I was getting too emotionally involved but I scoffed at his fear. I was a loving husband and a responsible father who could set limits to his relationships. I was also careful to delete any text messages that might make my wife uncomfortable. T

hree months into this relationship, Amaka called me that she wasn't feeling well and needed to see me. I promised her I will visit during my lunch hour. I went to the one-bedroom flat I had helped her to pay for.

There was nothing wrong with her. She told me she wanted to thank me in her own way for all the love and care I showed to her. I couldn't pretend not to understand her. Resisting her was futile and that was how I began to literally run two homes and have two personalities. She was fun to be with. And adventurous too. I had a new vitality that I didn't think possible. I started dressing better to impress her. I went weekly to the barbers' shop. I laughed at jokes that were not funny. I found my wife boring and tolerated her because of my children. Adaugo was just too staid and old-fashioned compared with this girl who set my whole body on fire whenever I met her. She knew how to please a man. Spending on her was a great pleasure which I couldn't equate with the new lease I had on life. I told her that if I had met her earlier, there wouldn't have been any Adaugo in my life. Her response baffled me.

"If you feel this way, we can still make it happen. She has two daughters, so it doesn't matter. I can have a son for you. She moves out while I move in and we will be happy together. You know you're happier with me than you are with her. Life is too short to be unhappy," she said and gave me a kiss.

How do I get rid of Adaugo? I couldn't say that I still loved her with the way my body was craving for Amaka, but I loved my daughters dearly. While we were together, I would be picturing how differently I would be feeling if it was Amaka who was with me. My wife had become boring, predictable, and not lively enough. In short, I found her presence a bit irritating. Our discussions seemed to center on money and bills to be paid. When last did she tell me that she loved me? When last did she notice how well I dressed? When last did she make an effort to wear what will turn me on? Her entire obsession was on how to get pregnant again and have a son for me. As if that was all that mattered to me.

Amaka asked detailed questions about my job, laughed at all my jokes, and kissed me on impulse. Amaka cooked delicacies with the money I provided and fed me with her hands. She would meet me at the door of her flat with a hug and in a crazy attire. This girl knows how to pamper a man and make him feel wanted.

Since our daughters arrived, my wife has been bogged down with caring for them that there was little attention for me. But I loved Somto and Ify. If I chose to break up with her, will they go with their mother? There's no how I will feel comfortable with my daughters sleeping elsewhere except under my roof. What will her family say? What will my own family say? I needed to man up and do the right thing. For my daughters and my family. This was the best time to run, and to run without looking back. This giddy delicious feeling was too good to be healthy.

I started avoiding Amaka. I stopped picking her calls. I stopped responding to her text messages. I tried to build it up with Adaugo again. I determined to pay her more attention. But I was miserable and irritable. I missed Amaka. I missed the feel of her body rubbing against mine. I missed her kisses. Even when I was with Adaugo I was thinking of her. It was like someone withdrawing from drugs and it was very difficult. It was affecting my concentration on the job and my colleagues noticed.

I had to go back to Amaka. Hopefully, the affair will die a natural death and my sanity will return. Time is the greatest healer. With time, the attraction will fade, but if it didn't, I will take only one step at a time. Maybe, I was cut out for a polygamous relationship. I rationalized it. Our forefathers were polygamous, and women didn't die. All men cheat, so why should it matter to Adaugo? Just provide well for her and the children and you are good to go. That's what a responsible father does. He's a financial provider. What he does with his life is his business. Why will I tie myself down with only *ogbono* soup all my life? Why not try, or continue with the *egusi*?

Variety is the spice of life. How many of my friends are faithful to their partners the way I have been all these years? In fact Adaugo should consider herself lucky. I wasn't chasing her away. I still loved her in my own way. I had decided that I needed a stable home, so I wasn't going to replace her. Amaka was just a side dish to amuse myself with.

The more I rationalized it, the less horrible it appeared. What of pregnancy? Not a bad idea. Amaka could have a son for me. Of course, I would hide his existence from my wife. No need to hurt her. But I would secretly be providing for Amaka and my son. He would be wild, adventurous, and masculine like his mother. I went back to the hide-and-seek game with Amaka. I changed the eateries we went to. I also stopped going to her house because a gossipy neighbor may find a way to tell Adaugo and I wasn't prepared for such a scandal. We met in different hotels for several months.

It happened while I was on my annual leave. One day after dropping my girls at school, I came home and had nothing to keep me busy. Adaugo had gone to her place of work. I heard a knock on our gate. I opened it to see Amaka. My first reaction was to tell her to go away, but she spoke first.

"I knew you would be all alone. Wife has gone to work. Children are in school. Father is on leave." I let her in quickly.

"You have a large and beautiful house and compound. Your wife is enjoying even when she can't give you a son."

"Don't talk about her like that," I scolded her. "That she hasn't given me a son yet doesn't mean that she can't."

She soft-pedaled immediately.

"I'm so sorry. I forgot that I'm just a girlfriend, not a wife! "Please, stop that. You know that I love you."

We went into the house.

CHAPTER 8

Adaugo discovers the infidelity

I WASN'T FEELING WELL AT ALL THAT DAY. AFTER SEVERAL VISITS TO THE restroom, my boss suggested I should go to the clinic. I told her I would prefer to go home, take some home remedies, and rest. I was given the rest of the day off.

It was good that Chukwudi was on leave. He will help me prepare food and also take care of our girls when they returned from school. I will pack my car outside so that Chukwudi would use it for school run. No need stressing myself to open or close the gate.

I got to our gate. The pedestrian entrance was not locked from inside. Was it Chukwudi who forgot to lock it from inside? How could he have forgotten?

I walked into the house. He must still be sleeping. Lucky man who's enjoying his leave. I opened our bedroom door. No, it's not real! I couldn't talk. My legs buckled under me. Chukwudi and the girl sprang apart. It couldn't have been me that walked back to the living room. It wasn't me that sat down on the settee.

I saw the figure of the lady, fully dressed now, walk hurriedly through the living room, through the courtyard and out of the gate. I didn't utter a word. What is seen can it ever be unseen? How do l wake up from this nightmare? Chukwudi! Where is Chukwudi? What explanation or apology was he going to offer?

Time stood still.

After what seemed like an eternity, Chukwudi came into the sitting room and knelt before me.

"I'm sorry, Adaugo. Really and truly sorry."

I shot him a murderous glance. No words. I couldn't frame any.

"You have every right to be angry," he started again, "but remember your children. They are the ropes around your waist."

"And did their father think of them before desecrating our matrimonial bed?" His ease of talking about it was aggravating. "Let me go and bring them back from school. Please try and act normal for their sake. We will sort out our lives later," he said and left.

This was the defining moment of our marriage. I was hurt. I was bitter. At first, Chukwudi was remorseful. He apologized over and over again, promised me that it will not happen again, and bought me gifts. But what I had seen kept replaying through my mind like an evil video produced by a malevolent spirit.

I didn't know how Chukwudi expected me to quickly sweep the experience under the carpet and pick back our relationship as if nothing happened. Would he have done so if the tables were turned? I asked him how he would have reacted if he had caught me red-handed in adultery. He responded that he would have divorced me. So how did he expect me to take what he himself wouldn't have endured? He said because I had more emotional strength and other wives had forgiven and moved on. He argued that he wasn't in love with Amaka and that what happened had nothing to do with his feelings towards me. Such a line of thought was simply exasperating. How do you cheat on someone you claim to love with someone you don't love? He said men were wired that way. But for a woman, adultery was preceded by emotional infidelity.

I felt like moving out, but I couldn't because moving out meant going back to my parents. And going back to my parents meant exposing my hurt and humiliation. I would have rented a place but I didn't have the money. I wept often. I antagonized him. I wanted to hurt him, to wound him, to retaliate in some way, but I didn't know what exactly to do to reward him for the pain he had inflicted on me. I moved out of the room which we shared. I contemplated getting a man, any man, as a lover to revenge the adultery, but I couldn't bring myself to do it. I berated myself for lacking the guts or the motivation. I doubted if cheating back would satisfy my desire for revenge. I couldn't describe the pain and humiliation which I felt to anybody, not because I respected my husband, but I didn't think anybody would understand.

I couldn't confide in Nma. She seemed to have her life on course. Her husband was doing well financially and they appeared to be very happy together. All my parents' initial doubts about Chukwudi came back to me. Did they really see beyond his façade? Was their instinct telling them that this smiling easy-going young man would cause their child this unbearable pain?

I decided against telling my mother. How would I describe what I had seen? Just reliving the scene was enough for tears to well up in my heart and eyes. I contemplated suicide, but I warned myself against doing anything that would hurt my daughters. It was obvious they didn't have a responsible father; so they needed a sane mother. They were the only considerations that held my riotous emotions in check.

When I wasn't healing fast enough, Chukwudi became insensitive and callous. He could go one whole week without speaking to me. He hurled accusations at me, telling me his adultery was entirely my fault. If I was a little more adventurous and if I dressed in a slightly crazier manner, he wouldn't have wandered from me. The accusation hurt as much as the deed itself. So what was I expected to do? Kneel and beg my husband to forgive me for making him cheat on me? How logical was that? He told me that he was no longer sorry. I should do my worst, after all, if I made the mistake of leaving home, several girls would joyfully take my place. This was like throwing a dagger at my heart.

I was losing weight. My marriage was crashing. No, it has crashed. Our once happy and joyous home was rife with animosity. Our daughters were frightened. They watched helplessly as their parents hurled painful words at each other. With time, I got to know the home breaker's name: Amaka. Amaka is the opposite of her name. Rather than bring goodness and beauty, she had cast gloom on my happy home.

My husband would leave the house in the middle of our quarrels. I didn't need a soothsayer to tell me where he went to. Sometimes, he would not come home late in the night and I would be left imagining what he would be doing with Amaka. Our situation was no longer a secret, even though our mutual friends avoided discussing it with me, I saw their sympathetic looks and it hurt. I had become an object of pity. Some friends who ventured broaching the topic suggested sending people to beat her up for destroying my home, but it didn't seem right to me. She doesn't owe me faithfulness. My husband does; and from the way he defended himself, I saw it wasn't just a fling. He was emotionally involved with her.

A physical confrontation was a no, no. What if she beats me up and injures me? I don't have respect for women who fight their husband's mistresses. If there's anyone to face, it is the husband. Others suggested meeting some pastors and native doctors. They believed firmly that Amaka had bewitched him. With proper intervention, the tie would be broken and he would come running back to you. Sounded too good to be true, but again not my nature. If someone doesn't voluntarily love me, I won't use fetish means to make him. I could try prayers, but nothing more.

Chukwudi was providing for the family, but I was too sad to notice. I tried to pull myself out of the depression but it was difficult. As he came back to us after a night out in his girlfriend's house, I had a long and bitter quarrel with him. He almost beat me up. After that, I cautioned myself against such since it didn't make any positive difference. We were no longer living like husband and wife but as sworn enemies.

He came home one Friday evening and packed some clothes in a bag and left. I didn't ask him where he was going and he didn't volunteer any explanation. I knew I had to go somewhere on that Saturday if I was to retain my sanity.

I dressed my girls and we went to the Amusement Park. As I watched them play with ropes, swing, and chatter, for once I felt peaceful. Returning to a lonely bedroom brought back the ache. On Sunday, I took them to church after which I visited Nma and her family. We chatted about the children, laughed at their baby talk, and discussed fashion trends. I was happy and relaxed. I told myself that I should be doing more of such. In the evening that Sunday, Chukwudi came back. I surprised myself by welcoming him at the door with a smile. I was actually relieved that he was safe. I was angry with him, but I didn't want him dead. "Did the girls ask of me?" "No."

"How did you spend your weekend?"

I told him about our visit to the park and how I spent part of my Sunday with my friends. He flew into a rage.

"Nobody cares about me in this house! You are poisoning the minds of my daughters. They don't love me. They don't care about me! Your husband traveled, but you don't care to know where he went and what he did. As long as I pay the bills, you are contented. I am the slave that labors to bring in the money. You moved out of our bedroom. You're the boss." I was surprised at the outburst. When I used to ask about his movements, he had told me it was none of my business. That as a man, he could go wherever he wanted and do what he wanted and I should live with it. Now that I didn't ask, he complained I wasn't loving or concerned.

But in his complaint, I saw a glimmer of hope: he seemed to care about my opinion and that of his daughters. I noticed he had asked Ifunanya whether I took them to see any 'Uncle.' My husband was jealous. He was worried that I may repay him with his own coin. I saw him eyeing me suspiciously and didn't know what to make of it. You were unfaithful to me but expect me to remain faithful to you. Talk of eating one's cake and having it! He must feel that in denying him of conjugal rights, I must be getting my satisfaction elsewhere.

We were very far from having a happy home again. I could see that he was conflicted. He wanted to pursue his passion for Amaka and at the same time enjoy a serene home with me. I was at the receiving end. Who would accept that?

A part of me wanted to stay put and watch how it played out. Another part yearned for a one thousand kilometer space between me and Chukwudi. But if I leave how would I be perceived? An irresponsible woman who abandoned her home and marriage for another woman. I bowed to societal pressure. "Don't allow another woman to reap the fruit of your labor. You knew Chukwudi when he had nothing. Now you have two cars and a good house. If you leave, the other woman will take over."

"Your family has no divorced woman. You can't bring such disgrace to them."

"Think of your daughters. Who will want to marry them if you separate from their father? They would have the stigma that their parents are separated."

"You must have let down your guard after delivery. Maybe you were tying wrapper and wearing a hair net inside the house. If you were dressing seductively, what would your husband find outside?"

"You were not prayerful enough. If you were more prayerful no strange woman would have come near your husband. Fire will consume such a woman."

"A good wife stands by her husband and doesn't let the devil tear her family apart. Wives must persevere. It doesn't make sense now, but in time, it will. Your character needs to be put to the test to develop your faith."

"If he's seeing another woman, *nko*? Did she carry him away? Doesn't he come back to you? You should be thankful for that. It is till death do you part."

"With all the options he has every day, you should be grateful that it's just one mistress."

The suggestions and pieces of advice were numerous. I wondered what the people would have advised the man if the tables were turned. Would they have blamed him for my committing adultery? Because that was the bottom line: I was the cause of Chukwudi's infidelity. I was too careless, prayerless, and tasteless in fashion and habits, and way too clueless to detect it. Nobody talked about my humiliation. It didn't matter that I was in agony. The intimacy and security I had with Chukwudi were gone. Our finances were also suffering. He threw it in my face that I earned so little. I would see heaps of receipts with Amaka's name on them. I could see that he furnished an apartment for her. Meanwhile, the fees for his siblings were unpaid and they were blaming me. I overheard one of them telling another that I 'ate' up their brother's money, but instead of adding weight, I was losing weight because of my evil heart.

Some men stop affairs when they are exposed or openly challenged. But after the initial unsuccessful apology, Chukwudi threw caution to the winds and dared me to do my worst. My daughters and I were at his mercy financially, and he knew it. He knew I would find it difficult to leave. My parents could offer some support but at this time, my loving father had retired from his salaried job and was collecting a meager pension.

I was experiencing bouts of sadness and irritability. Sometimes I would be talking to myself. I also had crying spells. A traffic warden once stopped me and I laughed like a maniac and he ran away. I contemplated suicide several times but felt too sorry for my daughters. I had to do something.

CHAPTER 9

Ifunanya notices the quarrels

I LOVE MY MUMMY AND MY DADDY. MY MUMMY IS VERY PRETTY. SHE takes good care of me and Somto. Sometimes, she buys the same material and makes uniform for herself, Somto, and myself.

She cooks delicious food for us. She's the best cook in all the world. She's also my best friend. She helps us with our homework. She's a very good woman.

My Daddy is the best Daddy in all the world. He calls me his Little Princess and Star. I like the pet names. He used to kneel on the floor and I would climb on his back and we would pretend that he's a horse and I am the rider. Somto would be laughing and clapping.

My Daddy is very wise. Even when I bring difficult homework, he would know the answer and show me how to do it. Sometimes, Daddy would come to my school to pick Somto and me after school. I like it when Daddy comes to pick us. He would stop at the ice cream shop and buy us ice cream and yogurt. Yummy!

He comes for our inter-house sports and I would run the sack race very well because I know my Daddy is seeing me and would be clapping for me.

My Mummy used to sing. While cooking, I would hear her sing. I used to also hear her singing in the bathroom.

But Mummy no longer sings. She's always looking sad. I opened the door of her room once and saw her crying. I told her I was sorry for annoying her, but she said it wasn't me. Then it must be Somto or Dad.

She wiped her face and tried to smile.

Daddy doesn't call me Little Princess anymore.

He doesn't ride horse with me anymore. As he comes into the house, he would frown and say, "Ifunanya, how was school today? Have you done your homework?"

Then he would enter his room, change from his work clothes, and leave the house. Somto and I are now afraid of Daddy and Mummy.

They were arguing in their room one day and I heard Mummy say Amaka was the cause of their quarrel.

Amaka! There is a girl called Amaka in my school. She's bigger than me. Otherwise, I would have fought her for making my parents quarrel. Maybe, I should report her to my teacher. My teacher said we shouldn't fight but report people to her.

I told my Mummy later.

"I heard that Amaka is making you and Daddy quarrel. I know her. I will report her to my teacher."

Mummy was surprised. "You know Amaka?" "Yes, she's in Primary 3."

Mummy burst out laughing. She said it wasn't that Amaka. Mummy is not happy. Daddy is not happy.

When we see Daddy's car at the gate, Somto and I would run to our room and hide. He acts as if he doesn't want to see us. When Mummy asks him for money to buy us things, he shouts at her.

One night, Mummy and Daddy were arguing as usual. Then I heard Mummy calling me and Somto. I was afraid. I thought she was going to beat us. We entered their room.

CHAPTER 10

Adaugo's desperate measure

Nma told me that she tried something which seemed to have worked with Alex. Unknown to her husband, she got a whiff that he was having an affair. She saw that she was losing him. He hardly had time for her and the children. He was staying late hours at work and excused himself by claiming he had business meetings; meetings which made him come home by 1 am. She reported to his elder brother, but he told her she should be contented with being the lady in the castle. For her sanity, she should look away. But she feared for infections and other associated issues like out-of-wedlock children.

In desperation, she decided to pray a strange prayer. She went to the back of her compound at midnight, stripped herself naked, and prayed, asking God to use any and every means to bring her husband to the path of rectitude. Not too long, Alex had a very close brush with armed robbers when returning by 1 am from those 'business meetings.' His car was riddled with bullets, but he sustained minor injuries. Anybody who heard of the incident queried him what type of meeting kept a married man out of his house till 1 am. They advised him to desist from such a lifestyle else he may not be lucky to survive it next time. He was ashamed and humbled.

He started coming home early. He enjoyed helping the children with their homework and Nma knew that the affair was over.

I decided to try this but in a different manner. I called my two daughters into the room to witness my last act of desperation. I stripped myself naked. Yes. Completely naked before my husband and my two girls.

He sat bolt upright in shock. The girls were scared to their bones.

"Chukwudi, you are the only man I've ever known and loved. I loved you as a teenager when I knew nothing about boys. Even when my parents persecuted me, I clung to the love I had for you. I didn't bother entertaining any other person because I knew it was you and you only that I have ever loved. When you graduated from the university and came to marry me, I accepted you. We had nothing but our dreams and love. I thought that we could build the empire of our dreams. Which girl would not want an elaborate fairy tale wedding, but I sacrificed my desires to accommodate your situation. I moved into a one-bedroom apartment because I believed in you and our greater tomorrow. True to your words, God has blessed us together. We have built our own house and have two cars. I have two daughters but you had told me it didn't matter to you. That God will still bless us with a son. I'm not earning much yet because I'm yet to secure my dream job, but whatever I am earning, I have always put back into our family to support you. What do I get in return for my love and sacrifice? Betrayal. Because of Amaka. You throw away our past because of Amaka. You use up our funds, funds we can invest in securing our future and the future of our children on Amaka. You sacrifice our children's happiness because of Amaka. Your family members are accusing me that you're no longer reaching out to them but they don't know that it's because of Amaka. When a man is good, he is naturally good but if he's not good, his wife made him. I am fed up by your attitude. I know what you're thinking. You want to frustrate me so that I will die and you can legally bring in Amaka. But you will not have your desire. I will not stay here and die or run mad. I am leaving you. But listen and listen carefully. If you bring Amaka to enjoy the fruit of my labor, I swear to you with my naked body and before our children that it will never be well with you and Amaka."

I dressed up calmly. When Chukwudi recollected himself, he was shouting at me.

"Adaugo, you cursed me! You cursed me with your naked body."

But I had nothing more to say. I told the children to go and pack their things. We were moving. My husband held them back.

"If you want to go, you can go. But my children are not leaving my house. I am their father."

I heard Ifunanya say "I don't want to go anywhere. I want to live with my Daddy and my Mummy."

Well, first things first. I needed space and time to regain my life. I drove out alone that night, back to my parents' house. My Mom was shocked to see me. I had been hiding from her since the situation in my marriage deteriorated. I had lost so much weight. She broke down in tears. My father was controlling himself. We all wept for a while until Mom asked:

"Where's Ify and Somto?"

"He insisted on keeping them."

They let me rest for three days, but as tradition demands, they reached out to Chukwudi's family for a reconciliatory meeting on the fourth day. A meeting that proved fruitless.

CHAPTER 11

Olanma the mother-in-law

SOME GIRLS DON'T WANT TO MARRY A MAN WHOSE MOTHER IS STILL ALIVE. What they don't know is that they are wishing themselves evil. Any girl who wants a dead mother-in-law will be dead before her own son marries. I am Chukwudi's mother. I was widowed early and I went through hell to raise him to become the man he is today.

I can never forget when he fell terribly sick at the age of six. He was admitted to the hospital. He had terrible pains on his stomach and the doctors didn't know what to do. Even as an adult, he still has that recurring pain, but it has never been as bad as that year.

At the hospital, the situation became very critical. My brother-in-law who was in the hospital with me while the father attended to the younger children at home had to go to our hometown some twenty miles away to make his yearly sacrifice to his ancestors. Since he was confident that I would soon return from the local market where I had gone to buy food-stuffs for our use and come to my son's bedside, he left him in the hands of the nurses. As I was told later, soon after he left, Chukwudi stopped breathing. The nurses packed his body and put it in the mortuary which then was just a slab.

When I came into the ward, I was shocked that the bed where the nurses had laid him was empty. I asked the nurses where they kept him. The nurses did not want to shock me with the sad news that he had died. They pointed to the mortuary, the ward they said they had transferred him to. Nobody told me that it was the hospital mortuary. There was no light there.

I was infuriated at what I thought was their heartlessness in putting a sick child in a ward where there was no light. I stormed into the ward angrily to take my child away from the hospital.

When I entered the mortuary, I saw him sitting up; something he had not done for months since the sickness started. He stretched out his hands to me. I picked him up but was shocked to see cotton wool in his nostrils and ears. I was angry the more regarding the way I felt the nurses had maltreated my son. I removed the cotton wool from his nostrils and ears, marched with him to the ward, and gave the astonished nurses a dressing down. I swore to them that I was done with their inefficient hospital and will never come there again.

It was in the process of narrating this experience to someone that I finally understood that my son had died and God had graciously restored him to life. Chukwudi is my special gift from God.

As he started school, he was showing so much promise. He was always coming first in his class. All the teachers liked him. In primary three, he had one particular teacher that took him as his child. Mr. Ugwu was very short. So short that the pupils had to stack up blocks for him to climb so that his hands could reach the top of the blackboard.

"You have somebody here," Mr. Ugwu told me of Chukwudi. "Every Naira you spend on him is a good investment."

His father died when he was still in secondary school. He had seven younger ones. But I wasn't going to let his huge potentials waste because of lack of money. I threw myself into raising the heir and hope of my family. I farmed crops. I fried and sold garri. I hired myself out as a daily farm labor hand. I sold my wrappers to raise money for his WASC fees.

I refused to admit other men into my bed. The men didn't want marriage. Who would marry such a liability as a widow with eight children? They just wanted fun but I turned down their advances. Even though my husband was dead, my eldest son was my husband and I respected him.

I dedicated my life to my children. Chukwudi continued to give me joy. He rushed through secondary school, had a very good result, and gained admission into the university. I don't know what it all meant, but I heard him say he got bursary and scholarship, so some people were paying his school fees and giving him money for food. God will bless those people because they made my burden lighter.

He graduated from the university. With pride, I heard people calling me 'Mama Engineer.' He soon got a job, and I was happy that I will finally rest and enjoy my son's money. I thought he would take off the load of raising his siblings from me.

But Chukwudi had his own plans. He told me that he wanted to marry. I was sad and unhappy.

"I thought you will marry us for some time before starting your own family."

I didn't want him to marry yet, but he pleaded with me to co-operate with him. The mother part of me was proud of him. This was a sign that he was a responsible man who didn't want to waste his earnings on random women.

When he brought Adaugo to show me, I liked her at first sight. I loved my son's choice. With time, she had two daughters. But, so what? Has she reached menopause? She will still give me lovely grandsons. I was proud of my pretty granddaughters who spoke good English. Adaugo was also doing well by me. She respected me. She bought me gifts. She did a little job and was helping Chukwudi with the training of his younger siblings.

It was from one of my children that I heard that Chukwudi was keeping a lady friend. I laughed it off. How many husbands are faithful to their wives? My generation was taught to overlook such things. We were told that men are polygamous by nature. Which man will be eating *ogbono* soup every day of his life? He will eat *egusi*, and vegetable for variety. A good wife will turn a blind eye so long as the man respects her and provides for her and his children. Monitoring a man was wrong. I was thinking of an opportunity to advise Adaugo, but I didn't know how she will take it. She may think that I was supporting Chukwudi whom I saw as just being foolish like other men. Here I was, a widow with eight children. Those who were asking me for a relationship were responsibly married men whose fine, young wives would have been shocked if they knew what the men were doing. Ignore him and after some time, he will get over his foolishness.

But this relationship didn't seem to be a passing phase. It was taking its toll on all of us. Fees for siblings were unpaid. Even the monthly support he and Adaugo were sending to me was no more regular.

I sent for my son. I told him to have patience, that Adaugo will give him a son. He told me he wasn't worried about a son. When I tried to enquire more deeply about what was going on, he flared up. He was a man! He earned his money and he could do whatever he liked with his money!

I backed down. I didn't want to annoy him more. He was our sole provider and I didn't want any woman to come between us. I was sure the outside lady was holding my son with a strong charm. Where do I go to release him? Was I the one who should be seeking a solution or should it be his wife? Some people suggested that I should consult a native doctor to bring his face back home, but God Who returned him to me after he had died, has the power to change everything. I will just pray and hope that they sort out their problems. I hoped that the affair with the outside lady will die a natural death and he will come to his senses.

Adaugo never reported him to me. I was her mother-in-law and maybe my earlier objection to their marriage made her not to fully trust that I was on her side, but God is my witness. I didn't send my son to commit adultery.

One Saturday, he came to see me. Adaugo had cursed him to his face with her naked body. That was an abomination! By doing that, she had ended the marriage herself. There will be no reconciliation. She had packed out of his house. She should have run to me and confided in me. She should have involved Chukwudi's uncles. How do you place a curse on your husband and the father of your children? Was she the only woman whose husband was unfaithful to?

I switched sides. No mother rejects her son, no matter what. I supported Chukwudi and whatever or whoever he thought was good for him.

CHAPTER 12

Amaka explains her own part

MY PARENTS HAD SIX OF US. NOT TOO MANY, YOU WILL SAY, BUT LIFE wasn't easy. They believed in giving us a good education. A university degree was the minimum. I was considered intelligent. I wrote WASC and UTME/JAMB once and secured admission into the East/West University. 'Bold and Beautiful' was my nickname. Campus life was sweet. I was finally free of parental control.

I had my first crush, a 300 level Political Science student. He 'disvirgined' me. Steve was all that a girl could ask for: six feet plus, athletic build, and rosebud lips. I was smitten. In my imagination, we were already married with three beautiful children.

The shocker came in my second year. That was when I understood that I was just a number, a game, a trophy, a piece of conquest. He had 'chopped,' cleaned his mouth, and was ready for the next trophy to be won. All his friends who had been calling me 'our wife' now called me either my first name or they avoided me altogether. They knew what he was doing.

Steve simply went missing in action. I tried to reach out to him but he told me that being in his final year, he was now too busy with his research project, seminars, and classes. It didn't take long before I noticed the object of his attention: a fresh, pretty innocent girl who was swooning over him. Steve went for the most beautiful of newly admitted girls. I thought of advising this girl, but I knew I would be accused of jealousy. She will learn the *use and dump* the hard way.

I suffered my first major heartbreak. I was depressed. Very depressed. Should I drink poison? But how would my poor parents feel? It wasn't my emotion alone that was battered but my finances too. Steve's parents must be rich because he had been spending heavily on me. I hardly asked my parents for anything and they always complimented me for being a good economical girl who managed with the little they were able to provide. I hid the truth from them. I kept all the costly crazy clothes and wigs that Steve bought for me with friends and went home on holiday with my old clothes. If only my parents knew.

My friends saw how downcast I was and told me the easiest way of getting over the heartbreak was to date other men. In fact, date multiple men. Why put all your eggs in one basket? If the men are not faithful, why should you be? One of them boasted to me that she had three men in her life: a campus toy-boy who paid for suya and occasional snacks and walked her to and fro lecture halls, a serious-minded man from her home town who was considering marrying her and a married man (an *Aristo*) who was picking her major bills. She called the married man her ATM. She was juggling her time among these three men and no one suspected her. Since the world was already spoilt I wasn't going to wage a one-woman war against it. I joined in the bandwagon. Love died with Steve. What mattered most was my survival.

Getting a boyfriend on campus wasn't difficult. He wasn't as handsome as Steve, but he was good company. I also got a fresh graduate who I was discussing settling down in the future with when his finances improved. I didn't want to tie myself with a married man, but occasionally I would go out with one or two to meet my financial needs.

I would occasionally surprise my parents with financial assistance. At first, my mother was wary how I got the money, but I told her that I was plaiting other female students' hair, I was making snacks and selling; I was going to Aba to buy bedsheets to resell. I indeed tried some of these things, but I got my bulk money from the men. I used to wince when I hear my mother proudly telling other mothers how industrious her undergraduate daughter was. She said I was so humble that I was combining trading with my studies just to make ends meet. She would say I wasn't like other girls who ran around with men just for money. She never suspected what I was doing.

As I rounded up my studies, a friend invited me to Alex's baby's naming ceremony. There I met Chukwudi. I could tell that he was fascinated by me. I sized him up. He looked financially comfortable. It didn't take long before I heard he had a house and two cars. Not bad for sugar daddy status. I made the first move and he fell for it. I didn't bargain for the emotion he was investing in the relationship. The closer we became, the more he was complaining about his wife. This was good for me. I could supply what he was missing in his marriage while he took care of my financial needs. It was a win-win situation. I didn't ask to replace his wife.

I graduated from university, but instead of going to my parents, I told them I needed to be in a town to secure employment. They readily agreed. I told my fiancé I would be staying with some friends. I did stay with a fellow girl for a short while, but Chukwudi soon rented a place for me. I was still in touch with my fiancé. He was sending money but not in the same way that Chukwudi was spending on me. My fiancé had told me that he was saving for our wedding ceremony.

Then Chukwudi's wife discovered us! I thought that would be the end of the relationship. He kept away from me for some time but returned with greater ardor. I was confused. I feared for my safety if the angered wife would bring some thugs to beat me up. But Chukwudi assured me that she could never do that. I feared her going diabolical on me but he told me I was just being superstitious. Foolish wives have always been replaced with younger, scheming girls and the heavens didn't fall. He was also spending heavily on me. Whatever I demanded, he made efforts to supply. I wasn't ready to let go of the relationship anytime soon. I let go of other men and concentrated on him and my absent fiancé. Before my wedding, I would gradually ease him off and be a virtuous wife to my husband.

He had discussed the possibility of marrying me, but I didn't believe that he would really leave his wife and children and come to me. Several times, my conscience pricked me. 'You're destroying another woman's home. You're a husband snatcher. You're depriving those girls of their father's affection.' But I rationalized it. I didn't snatch him. Who snatches an adult? I didn't kidnap him. He chose to come to me. I didn't force him to be spending on me. He chose to do so. I didn't rob him, neither did I snatch his money at gunpoint. If a wife is not careful with her possession, she shouldn't blame another person for collecting it.

Chukwudi was keeping me abreast of developments in his home. One day, he announced to me that his wife had moved out in anger. I saw he was happy, so I tried to look happy too. 'The girls will miss their father,' I pretended to be concerned.

"No, they will miss their mother," he corrected me.

It hit me! He had collected his daughters from his wife. And he was asking me to move in with him. This was much more work than I had bargained for. With no prior experience of childbirth and childcare, I was going to be a mother of a five-year-old and a three-year-old.

"Shouldn't you have allowed them to go with her?" I asked. "My children live with me and that's final. But you had told me it didn't matter that I had two daughters. You will definitely have a son and we will be happy together."

I weighed my options. He was spending on me in a way my fiancé couldn't. I wouldn't say that I was really in love with my fiancé but he was my backup plan to ensure that I got married. He was the only man that had shown the intention of making me his wife and I wasn't going to throw him away until I got a better alternative. Luckily, he was too busy at work to pay me visits. He was also living in a town, eight hundred kilometers away from where I was. I had also told him that I covenanted with my Maker that there will be no sex before marriage since I was still a virgin. We agreed to keep ourselves for ourselves till that special day. I had already worked out the story to tell if he found out that I was otherwise on our wedding day. I would tearfully tell him how I was raped by a cousin who threatened me that I would die if I let out the secret. In my naivety, I agreed with my cousin. What did I know?

But moving in with a married man was another issue altogether. I worked out the plan for that. I told my fiancé that my uncle from my mother's side had invited me to assist him to take care of his young daughters because his wife was traveling abroad. They believe I am so wonderful with children that she left her two daughters for me. I am those girls' favorite aunt so they won't miss their mother at all.

My fiancé was happy.

"I know how much you love children. Don't worry. We shall soon get married and you can have half a dozen of your own," he teased me.

I also told him that I was relieved that I was moving over to my uncle's because armed robbers were terrorizing our neighborhood, so my uncle's place was safer than where I was. My parents still believed that I was with a friend looking for a job. Nobody suspected anything.

I needed Chukwudi's money and he needed me. So I moved in. I will take life one day at a time. Whatever will happen should happen. I stayed indoors most of the times. Here, I was a mother of two girls who didn't hide their resentment of me.

I remember entering the house and Ifunanya asked her dad who I was.

"That's your new mother. Her name is Amaka. But you must call her Mummy."

"But I don't like her. I won't ever call her Mummy. She's not my mummy."

Even though I was angry, I really couldn't blame the poor child.

The few neighbors that saw me cast disdainful glances in my way, and I would hear 'Home Wrecker.' This happened on the times I opened or closed the gate for Chukwudi to move out or come in. I was literally under house arrest. He couldn't take me out or introduce me to his social circle. No member of his family visited us. I declined any such publicity even when he suggested it. I mustn't jeopardize my prospects of marrying honorably. I was cooking and cleaning for him and his children.

In less than one month, Chukwudi and I started having misunderstandings. I discovered that he wasn't as rich as I had imagined. I had to beg for very simple things like money to go to the hair salon. I had expected that he would welcome me with a car. The day I mentioned it, all hell was let loose.

"I'm not a thief. I am an ordinary salary earner. I also have siblings that I'm paying for their education."

That shut me up, but I wasn't happy. I seemed to be the last of his priorities now that I was in his house.

Maybe, I should have remained a mistress instead of . . . instead of what? Exactly what was my status?

He hadn't legally or officially married me. So I wasn't a wife. I started feeling like a glorified house girl. It was more fun catching our cruise from afar. He was more caring then than now when we were living together. His whole attention was on his daughters. When I asked for money for a wig, I was told Ify's fees will be paid, Ify's lesson fee was due. Ify! Ify! I felt that even though the mother had left, she kept a version of herself to torment me. Chukwudi was always rushing to her defense as though she was my co-wife.

One day, as usual, Ifunanya was giving me an attitude. I flogged her. When Chukwudi came back from work, I reported to him, and he supported his daughter. He told me that I was wicked. I should put myself in the little girl's shoes. She's only a child and was missing her mother. I told him that I didn't drive her mother away. He did.

He argued that I made him to. He was blaming me for his decision to wreck his marriage. That was taking matters too far and I wasn't going to accept it. How would a mature consenting adult not take responsibility for his decisions and bear the consequences of those decisions? I made up my mind on the next steps. My business is to look out for my own interest.

CHAPTER 13

Obuora on fatherhood

FATHERHOOD! NOTHING PREPARES ONE FULLY FOR THE INEXPRESSIBLE JOY counterbalanced with the unspeakable anguish that accompanies being a father. I'm expected to be a provider, protector, leader, disciplinarian, and best friend. Yet all the accolades of parenting go to the mother. There are more emotional quotes dedicated to the mother than to the father.

Who sat and watched my infant head
When sleeping on my cradle bed
My Mother.

Songs are written in her honor. Nico Mbarga's classic is sung every Mother's Day bringing up emotions of tenderness:

Sweet mother I no go forget you For de suffer wey you suffer for me

When I no chop my mother no go chop When I no sleep my mother no go sleep She no dey tire

When I no well my mother go carry me She go say instead I go die make she die She go beg God

God help me, my pikin.

Where are the songs for the fathers? The children seem so attached to their mothers. When they grow up, they buy gifts for her and they share their secrets. Beyond picking the bills, will my family miss me?

Early in life, I decided my home will be different from the one I grew up in. If my father loved my mother, he never showed. We thought of him as a tyrant who unleashed undue punishment and terrorized his household. Over the years, my impression of him had changed and I had come to appreciate a man who did only what he considered his best for his family's good. My siblings and I were doing well, so maybe, the strict discipline was worth it, after all. Age had also mellowed him. He sought for closeness with us and asked our opinion on issues, but it couldn't fully undo the havoc of our growing up years.

I plan to be really close to my children. I want them to love me and relate to me. I had long decided to be an involved father, to have the kind of relationship I wished my own father had with me. I will do bicycle races, play ball and attend school events for my children.

Nkechi, my wife and the mother of my children, calls me her Rock of Gibraltar. That's one appreciative woman. She thinks that I am steady and dependable. Unknown to her, I am plagued with self-doubt and insecurity just like every other person. But I have to act tough.

I worry about not being a good provider. I wish I could do more financially but as an averagely paid civil servant, there's a limit to what I can do. Nkechi is a primary school teacher working with the Ministry of Education and with our combined earning, we manage to keep our little clan going.

I am saddened by the apparent collapse of Adaugo's marriage. If they follow through with a divorce, I would be stripped of my knighthood in church. I won't be an example of a Christian father who has well-behaved children. It may even affect the chances of her younger ones marrying from respectable Christian homes. Parents are blamed for the moral failure of their children. It's assumed that they didn't do their duty well, which is why their children's marriages collapsed. Where will I hide my shame?

I know I did a fantastic job with Adaugo. This is one child who had not caused me any unnecessary anxiety. She was not strong-headed or rebellious. How she managed to be the one experiencing difficulty in holding her home together was beyond my understanding.

I had seen the signs of trouble long before that night when she returned home. Living in the same town meant that we bumped into each other frequently; at family functions and other social events. When she started sending apologies for absence instead of attending, I knew that she was purposely avoiding me. What had transformed my once happy child into this frightened, vulnerable woman? My wife and I hadn't had such travails in our own marriage. Ours wasn't perfectly alright. We had our own share of misunderstandings and uncomfortable moments, but communication never broke down to the extent of her packing out and leaving home. I remember refusing her food on some occasions and she would invite her mother to come and beg me. It all felt so foolish now. How could I reject food in my house because I am angry with my wife? First, the wife is mine. Second, the food is mine. Third, the anger is mine. So whatever I chose to do with these three things was up to me. These days, I choose to transfer the anger to the food and eat it angrily!

Our marriage was arranged by our parents. Or to put it better, they chose for us and we ratified their choice. Our success so far makes me wonder which type of marriage works better. Our parents chose for us and we entered into the marriage with each being aware of their roles and responsibilities in the marriage. These younger ones claim to fall in love, marry for love, and then discover that love alone cannot sustain a marriage. It is old fashioned commitment and patience that has kept us going these many years.

I had graduated from university and secured a job when my father told me that he had seen a good girl that will make a good wife. He had sounded her family too and they were not opposed to the plan. I clenched my teeth. What if I didn't love her? What if she was ugly and timid? But I asked the most worrisome question.

"I hope she's not a nurse," I queried. "No." She's in a teacher training college."

I loved that. Other men could marry nurses but not me. No wife will be going for night duty from my house. I always wanted to marry a teacher who will have time for the home. I also heard that teachers' children are usually brilliant.

"If you see her and you don't like her, you know that nobody will force you," that was my father.

I visited her at school and I was impressed. In the course of our short discussion, I could see that she was attractive, smart, and funny. Being a teacher and a first daughter meant that she will be caring and would definitely add value to my life. She responded to my questions with neither timidity nor brashness. I loved her appearance too. I was ten years older than her. Just the right age gap. I wasn't too near her age for her to disrespect me. Neither was I too old for her to fear me as a father or an uncle. The fact that my family accepted her, in fact, chose her for me, was a bonus.

I proposed, and with joy, she accepted. We got married in a lavish ceremony that was the talk of the town for quite some time.

While I wouldn't have minded if she didn't get pregnant immediately, I was elated when she informed me that I was going to be a father a month after our wedding.

"Your own is a magnet," my fellow men teased me.

"You're a sharpshooter. You shoot without missing your target."

It was gratifying to know that I had such power between my loins.

Adaugo arrived! I know every parent thinks their child is the best, but the truth is that she was the prettiest and smartest child that I had ever known or seen. She had such healthy lungs that her screams could be heard from afar. She also had a good appetite. Within those few weeks, I think she ate longer than she slept.

I enjoyed being a father. She burped and poured breast milk over my neck while I massaged her back and I enjoyed it. While trying to change her nappy, she pooped on my trousers and it was all fun. I was smelling like a nursing father.

I updated my records in my place of work. Under the space for dependent children, I wrote her name in full 'ADAUGO OBUORA.' The next question was the profession. What should be written as a baby's profession? I wrote 'Town Crier.'

About six weeks after her birth, I left my two angels to fight in the Civil War. I carried their pictures in my mind while doing sentry in the trenches. The hope of the glad reunion with my family kept me alive and sane amid hunger, sickness, and depression. I had vivid dreams of them which I relived in my waking moments to keep me going. The details of the dreams were always the same: a return to my job and my home with beautiful Nkechi and Adaugo cuddled up in my arms as we shared intimate moments in bed. I would wake up to the sound of mortar, bullets, the rations of poor quality food, the shrieks of the dying, the anguish of the wounded, the gory sight of those who had been shredded by mines and machine guns. One day this nightmare will end. The dreams gave me hope that my family was still alive and that we will be reunited one day.

We survived the war and were indeed reunited. My wife was like a virgin all over. I had thought that drastic changes would have happened to her as a result of pregnancy and childbirth, but I was wrong. I was also glad that Nkechi had not sold herself cheaply to soldiers or any available male for food, shelter, or protection. She had kept herself for me.

It was a pleasure watching Adaugo grow. After her initial hesitation, we soon became the best of friends. Uncountable packets of biscuits, lollipops, chewing gums. Different types of toys: dolls and teddy bears. She was their mother and I joined her as we gave the dolls names. I bought her toys: cooking and sewing sets and enjoyed her play make-believe chef. I provided her with whatever a little girl would desire. I bought storybooks and read them to her. Her eyes were wild with the magic of Cinderella, Snow White, Rapunzel, and Sleeping Beauty. She wore fancy clothes and was registered at a good Nursery/Primary school. My wife often jokingly complained about having a rival.

"Adaugo, leave my husband and go and marry your own," she teased her.

"But Daddy is my husband."

As a child, she didn't enjoy dinner if I wasn't around. I helped her with her homework. I nursed her when she fell sick. I remember when she was so ill that she threw up the cereal I had fed her on my new shirt. She was apologetic but I told her that it wasn't her fault. All she needed to do was to get well quickly.

Sweet little girls refuse to remain little. Before my eyes, she transformed into a stunningly pretty teenager. She began to hide from me to dress up. She insisted on her brothers knocking on her room door before entering. Her taste in storybooks changed. She wanted stories of romance, of marriage and 'they lived happily ever after.' Then I began hearing of love letters. My initial reaction was fright. Who's this enemy that wants to spoil my young sapling? I was murderous! But my wife assured me that no damage was done.

She continued with her education and I was proud of her. After graduation, she presented Chukwudi as a suitor. I was happy that my product had a market value, but I had been dreaming of her marrying a man who was more comfortable financially instead of the first son of a widow who had numerous siblings to cater to.

"Apart from his having a poor mother, what are your other objections?" she had asked.

"None, if you think that he will make you happy," I had told her.

"Chukwudi is my first and only love, Daddy. He is the only man I have ever wanted to marry."

"I hope you don't regret this decision," I insisted.

I didn't want to hear stories tomorrow. She shouldn't marry in haste and spend the rest of her life regretting her decision. If she would exercise patience, a more comfortable suitor may show up. How many years would they spend raising seven younger siblings before they can focus on building their own financial future? I am not unduly materialistic but money matters in marriage. I have seen marriages that crashed because of money for house upkeep.

"No, Daddy. I won't regret following my dreams by marrying Chukwudi. I know that we are starting small, but we don't despise the days of little beginnings."

I noticed that my daughter was already using 'we' in referring to herself and Chukwudi. Her mind was made up. She had outgrown my love or rather expanded the love she had for her family to accommodate another person. My girl was yearning to leave the nest, to fly, and to start her own life independent of us.

She gave me one parting shot:

"I think you're jealous, Dad. You don't like another person taking me away from you," she was winking at me.

"You're right, my Ada. It's like losing you, and to an inferior person," I wasn't as amused.

"Chukwudi isn't inferior to you. He may not be rich, but he's ambitious and hard-working. Besides, you're not losing a daughter. You are gaining a son."

"Amen! May it be so. I brought you up well and trust that you will make the right decisions."

Out of the love I have for her, I accepted Chukwudi as a son. I also bent over backward to plan their wedding and marriage with them. I would have liked to host a big wedding party for my first child who was getting married, but they declined. I argued that it would seem as if she was pregnant out of wedlock and that her wedding was a hushed-rushed event to cover up, but they were adamant. They wanted a small party and I convinced my kinsmen to let them have their way. The couple desired a simple ceremony and I stood by them. I knew that it was Chukwudi's ego at play. He didn't have the means for a lavish party and didn't want me to pay for it so that he won't feel obliged to me.

Adaugo made me a young grandpa and I was overjoyed. I loved playing with my two adorable granddaughters. They were doing well financially too. They changed accommodation from one small space to an even bigger one until they moved into their own house.

A while later, I started noticing cracks. I saw her grappling with the challenges of keeping her home. I didn't want to be accused of being an interfering or nosy parent so I tried to keep my distance. I am to remain an in-law, not an 'outlaw.' But inwardly, I was deeply perturbed. She was sickly and sad and I was powerless to do anything about it. My daughter's happiness lay in another person's hands and I could see her suffering. Why can't I change the hand of the clock? Where is the smiling girl who wrote me heart-warming messages on Fathers' Day? I kept those cards and re-read them from time to time. Another man was causing her grief and I couldn't confront or challenge him lest I hurt my already hurting child. She came back to us. Outwardly, I seemed to be angling for her home to be reunited, but inwardly I was relieved that she was alive and well under my roof. She needed to be alive before being married.

In the course of her stay, I found out that it was the intrusion of another woman into her home that caused the breakdown. Was it nemesis? Were my sins coming to haunt my daughter? Was it payback time? I had strayed twice in the course of my own marriage. A married colleague in the Ministry of Finance. This was against my father's warnings. He had asked me to steer clear of married women that they would bring me nothing but wound and dishonor, but Kate was difficult to resist. She seemed to want me as much as I wanted her. Stolen waters are sweet and bread eaten in secret seems to taste better. I think the sense of danger heightened the adventure. The affair was discreet. I made sure that Nkechi never suspected anything. I was nicer to her at home than usual and gave her more gifts than before.

"My husband, you're in love with me all over. All these Darling and Sweetheart that you're calling me. Plus the gifts too. Other men should come and learn how to be a good husband from you. If there's another world, wait for me because I would still marry you."

My secret was safe. I was using the gifts to silence the periodic guilt that I felt.

Nothing lasts forever. Kate and I split after we narrowly escaped being discovered by a cleaner while making out in the office toilet. We just dodged a bullet! The scandal that would have rocked our two families would have destroyed us, especially Kate. Which husband forgives an adulterous wife? Her husband is on a larger and sturdier frame than me. I imagined him charging at me with a machete in his hand. Kate and I agreed that our foolishness must end.

But temptations come over and over again and despite our best resolutions, we find ourselves enmeshed in unplanned relationships. This time, the temptation came in the form of a young, unmarried lady. I was even more careful to cover my tracks. The affair would have continued for a longer period because unlike that of the married woman, I wasn't feeling guilty relating to a free consenting adult. I knew that I was betraying Nkechi, but I was a responsible father who was providing whatever was needed by his household. It didn't even reduce the love I have for her. Tina was just a toy, an insignificant diversion from the monotony of monogamy. We avoided discussing my family. It was none of her business. She once made a disparaging remark about wives who allowed themselves to age prematurely and wouldn't take care of themselves pushing their husbands to more desirable women. I saw it as a veiled reference to my wife and warned her sternly never to talk about such in my presence. She backed down and if she ever mentioned my family at all, it was with respect. I was spending on her, but I made sure that it wasn't at the expense of my family.

One day, Tina came to see me in the office.

"Thanks for all the love you've shown me. I want to let you know that I'm getting married."

I couldn't believe my ears. It was as if I was hit by a trailer carrying cement. I realized I had grown fond of her. She wasn't intrusive, neither did she try to run my life. She was just a dependable and discreet person whom I spent idle moments with.

"You can't do this to me!" I managed to blurt out.

"Do what, Sir? You are married with your own children and you expect me not to start a family of my own? I know that you can never marry me. I didn't know you would be this selfish," she countered me.

"Me, selfish! When I have been spending on you." "But you can never be my husband," she argued. "Let me marry you and keep it a secret," I offered.

"Will you advise Adaugo your daughter to do the same thing? Why will I marry an old man like you when there's a young man of my age willing to marry me? Our relationship is a business relationship: you wanted fun and I needed money. Now that I have a better offer, I will move on. I can't sacrifice being a first lady to be a snack for an ancient man who may retire and die soon. Goodbye, Sir." And she left.

I fell sick. I lost appetite. My wife was worried about me, but I couldn't disclose the real cause of my ailment, so I allowed her to treat me for nonexistent malaria. Tina passed by my office and dropped her wedding card with my clerk. She was avoiding me. She wanted to safeguard her new relationship from any possible scandal emanating from her past. How dare she? After all the expenses on her! Did she expect me to attend? It will be like watching my wife marrying another man. I felt that she was unfaithful to me. We were lovers for crying out loud. But she had betrayed me and moved on.

I came to my senses about a month later after dispassionately reviewing the relationship. My ex-mistress was right. I was the selfish person who ate my cake and still wanted to have it. Her question had given me considerable pain:

"Will you advise Adaugo to marry an old man and be hidden from being acknowledged as his wife?" No. I wouldn't have advised my daughter to accept the status of a second wife to a civil servant on the verge of retirement. I felt remorseful. I was the one who had taken advantage of Tina's youth and neediness. It must not happen again.

I came back to Nkechi psychologically and emotionally and threw myself into loving her fervently. I had betrayed her without her knowledge, but I knew she had been true to me. It's surprising that I could have a tryst with a married woman, but still firmly believe that my wife was incapable of doing the same. I promised myself that I will never stray again. There was no point in confiding my previous failures to my wife. What you don't know won't hurt you. The main point was to move forward without looking back.

I did attend Tina's wedding. I bought her a gift. I went with Nkechi to the event. Tina appeared pleasantly surprised to see us. Without any telltale signs of our past liaison, and without as much as batting an eyelid, she introduced me to her groom as one of her uncles who had shown her kindness. Women!

When my daughter's marriage fell apart, I felt that this was God's punishment to me. Talk of fathers eating sour grapes and children's teeth being set on edge! Because in my mind, I could see no way that Adaugo merited the crisis she was in. But I hadn't broken any homes. I only strayed for some time and returned to my family.

I put emotions and guilt-trips away and faced the practical task of rehabilitating her emotionally and financially. Even though I had retired from the civil service, I had good connections that came in handy. We paid for her to take some certification courses on editorial writing. The state radio corporation advertised and she was hired. I heaved a sigh of relief. She will be able to take care of herself better. At least financially.

Her confidence level rose. With time, I saw my darling girl joke and laugh once more.

CHAPTER 14

Adaugo experiences healing

THE SEPARATION FROM CHUKWUDI ALLOWED ME TIME TO REFLECT ON MY life and marriage. I was bitter. Very bitter. I was angry with Chukwudi. I felt used and abused. I was missing my daughters. Terribly. I couldn't say how well they were being taken care of. I feared that Chukwudi may have dumped them with his mother in the village because I couldn't see how he will cope with taking care of them and giving his best at work. If he sent them to live with his mother, how would the girls transition from city children in a good nursery school to village girls? How about feeding? Will they be given *garri* and soup three times a day as I had often seen Lady Mother-in-law eat? Were they properly bathed or will they develop eczema and ringworm as I had seen other children? How about their school work? How well will they perform if they are sent to public ill-equipped schools? Taking my darling girls from me was the most wicked act that Chukwudi had ever done. It pained as much if not more than desecrating our matrimonial bed. If only I had my daughters around me, I could face their upbringing and forget about him. I would pour all my love on them. My poor innocent children were the casualties of this war between their parents.

Here I was at my parents' house. I was well-fed, pampered, and petted without knowing anything about my daughters' welfare. I was weeping so much about them that my mother surreptitiously sent people to Okiti to find out about them. They were not in the village with Lady Mother-in-law. I was relieved. At least, he must be caring for them by himself. But how was he managing?

I hoped he didn't bring a male relative into the house. Since I had daughters, I didn't approve of male relatives coming for long periods of stay in our house. I had heard that a good number of little girls were sexually abused by male relatives and I had been very protective of my daughters. He may have brought a house girl. Remembering my experience with Rose, it's akin to say that he had married a second wife. I can almost be certain that my husband would sexually abuse a house girl. Such thoughts drove me to the point of insanity and thoughts of suicide crossed my mind several times. If I couldn't protect my children, why was I alive?

I had experienced the shock of Chukwudi's betrayal.

Processing the experience over and over moved me to anger at all men who spend time to woo you, only to betray your trust in such a shameless manner. Men are scum. I railed at the universe. I cursed fate that made me meet such a heartless fellow like Chukwudi. I extended the anger to my parents. They should have exercised their parental authority and stopped me from marrying him. It would have hurt, but I would have obeyed them and spared myself this trauma.

My father reminded me that I was the one that insisted, but I was still feeling that they were to blame. My mother especially. I heard that mothers can instinctively assess people. Why didn't she assess this man and warn me? My parents had a good marriage and I was the one suffering. It was so unfair.

My parents were patient with me. They didn't mind my outbursts. They continued showing me unconditional love.

Then one day, I saw the need to move on. I sat down and reasoned long and hard with myself. If I continued the way that I was going and ended up dead or in a psychiatric hospital, my parents would have lost a daughter, my daughters would have lost a mother and my death would not restore my broken home. If anything, Chukwudi would bring in his mistress or another woman and continue with his life.

I willed myself to live. I willed myself to move on. For myself. For my parents. For my daughters. I started looking for help, for anything that will put me on the path of recovery and healing.

I read an extract that literarily opened my eyes and spoke to my innermost being. It sounds like what was written by a fellow woman with a similar experience:

If you are tired of feeling like a victim, read this: "I don't want to feel this way anymore. I thought if my pain touched their lives . . . if they acknowledged how wrong they've been I'd feel better. . . . I read books and talked with counsellors. . . . Finally I did two things that worked . . . I decided to forgive and keep forgiving . . . Second, I cried out to God."[1]

I read this extract more than twenty times. I read it so many times that I was reciting it by memory. More than reading it, I decided to put it into practice. It would be unfair to me to keep harboring anger, suicidal thoughts, and bitterness while my husband and his mistress were enjoying their lives. My best revenge was to let go of resentments and rebuild my life. I didn't want to be a victim any longer. I read a quote on anger and malice—that it's like drinking poison while hoping the other person would die. I was killing myself by myself! I wasn't going to continue that way. I decided to change and there was no going back. Once the bitterness crossed my mind, I remembered the drill: forgive and ask God for grace. So I would tell myself, sometimes talking loudly "I forgive Chukwudi and Amaka." Next, I would whisper a prayer asking God to work on my attitude. I would immediately feel lighter and better.

I pushed away depressive thoughts from my mind and I brushed away humiliating feelings. I chose not to ruminate on negative feelings. I started exercising my body. It was a great mood lifter.

I reconnected with my old school friends. I had been avoiding them. I had thought that they would ostracize me for having a broken marriage, but they rallied around me. The encouragement was overpowering. I discovered that my experience wasn't peculiar to me. Some of my fellow old girls were going through similar betrayals. We talked about them. We laughed at ourselves. We put loud music, and danced like teenagers. We took turns to host each other. It was almost sinful feeling as free as we were. My youthful looks returned. I was healthy and happy.

Then it seemed as if a pack of wolves were released on me! Men! Young men came prophesying undying love. Widowers came begging me to come and keep them company. Gigolos looking for a free meal. It was difficult keeping to myself. But I knew where my heart was: with my first love and the father of my children. It was difficult not to think of him. I railed at him publicly, but I knew that if he looked in my direction again, I

1. See Gass, "Are You Feeling Like a Victim?"

would follow him without a moment's delay. My heart was still beating for him and him only.

I inwardly blamed the Amaka girl. It must be her fault. She must have enticed him in a way that he couldn't resist. If only he had confided his challenges to me. We would have worked out a solution instead of throwing away all we shared and worked for. Like most wives, I made excuses for my husband and blamed the intruder. She should have known better than wrecking a fellow woman's house. I excused my husband. Maybe, just maybe there were things I didn't get right. Maybe I should have handled things differently. I should have controlled my anger. Cursing him with my naked body must truly have been weird and esoteric. He said he was in doubt of my sanity. Who wouldn't be after such a display?

Apart from that, I couldn't find any other fault with my conduct as a wife. Some of my friends said that maybe I was not dressing seductively enough. I looked through my wardrobe. I didn't think that was the problem. I had decent clothes, appropriate for a married woman to wear without looking like a low budget prostitute. I had tried one of that bizarre lingerie with Chukwudi and rather than being excited, he had been shocked. In whispers, he asked me where I had bought such indecent clothes from. He warned me against friends who will sway me from being the decent virtuous woman that he had married. He said if he needed a wild woman, he wouldn't have married me. So how come it's now my inability to spice up my wardrobe with 'for him only' clothes that was now the issue? I didn't think so.

I respected his family and didn't interfere, no matter what he spent on them. I sent my own little support. If his siblings do well and were in good positions, not only will they not be a liability to us, they might assist us if we bumped into rough times in the future. So in building them, we were investing in our secure future.

A few of them who genuinely loved me made out time to visit me in my parent's house. Uche, his younger sister, was my favorite among his siblings. She began living with us right after we got married. We had our fair share of in-law squabbles, resolved them, and became best of friends. At first, she wanted me to know that the house was her brother's house. She refused to help out with housework. Chukwudi noticed and ordered her out of the house, never to come back. She wept bitterly and accused me of poisoning her brother's mind against her. Rather than join issues with her,

I waited for her anger to die down. I sat down with her and explained to her where she wasn't doing well. She apologized and by the time Chukwudi came back from work the next day, we were chatting and cooking together. He was surprised and also relieved. Now in my trying period, Uche who was now an undergraduate visited frequently and reassured me that things will still normalize between her brother and I. She had boycotted his house since he brought in the 'strange woman.'

I refused to open my mind to admit another man. I was faithful to Chukwudi even after we had separated. It didn't have to do with the children. I was imprisoned by my love for him. Talk of Stockholm Syndrome. That was the real rope around my waist. I couldn't admit another person into my heart. Maybe later, but not just yet. My admirers hit at my weakest point: he treated you like trash. True. But I still love him.

One of my old girls told me about training for editors organized by some experts. My mother helped me pay for it and shortly after the training, I secured my first real career job with a media outfit. I was earning a salary way beyond my imagination. My confidence level skyrocketed. I was empowered. The job was good for me. I was working on shifts.

I found out that Chukwudi didn't change school for my children. He kept them in the same school. If I couldn't come to the house to see them, no law prevented me from seeing them at school. I started visiting them regularly at school. I would go during their lunch break to avoid meeting Chukwudi when he came to drop or pick them from school.

The first visit was a very emotional one for me. My girls squealed with delight and threw themselves at me. I wept and laughed at the same time. I gave them food. It was break-over but the girls clung to me, making me very sad. But I told them that all would be well. I would be visiting them more regularly. It was Ifunanya that told me that Amaka had moved in. I had anticipated it but it still hurt to know that Chukwudi had replaced me with her. I was near tears again but I remembered: forgive and ask for the grace to manage your attitude. I breathed forgiveness in their direction and did the practical thing.

I encouraged my daughter to obey her and try to respect her. Managing my hurt will come later.

"Mummy, I asked her to help me with my homework, but she said I am foolish like my mother. That if you weren't foolish, Daddy wouldn't have sent you out. I told her you are not foolish."

I felt the anger mounting. But I reminded myself. No anger, no resentment.

"Bring the homework let me help you." I put her through.

Somto was the worse. After every visit she would ask me, "Mummy, are you coming home with us?" If only adults knew the agony they put children through with their choices, they will not do such silly things. But humans are essentially selfish. They consider only their emotions.

One day, I went late to our lunch break appointment. I knew my daughters will be expecting me that day and I didn't want to disappoint them. I rushed to their school to give them their lunch, a hurried embrace, and then zoom off.

Then I saw Chukwudi. Our eyes met for a few seconds. He was gaping at me. I entered the car.

"Bye, children. See you later."

Alone in my office, I analyzed the look. It wasn't disdain. It was surprise. Not an unpleasant surprise. I faced my work. Whatever he felt was entirely his business.

CHAPTER 15

Chukwudi and Amaka co-habit

I WAS EXCITED THAT AMAKA ACCEPTED TO MOVE IN AFTER ADAUGO moved out. Threatening me while completely nude was scaring. I mean, who does that? And she did it before our daughters. What impression would that leave with the children? In fact, I was doubtful of her sanity, a major reason for taking the children from her. If she was so emotionally volatile, who says she cannot harm herself and the children. Other women knew their husbands kept mistresses. Why would mine go overboard?

She should understand that it's a man's world. It crossed my mind that she could retaliate. Can Adaugo commit adultery? The thought filled me with revulsion. I will kill her and kill the man. Funny how we expect other people to endure what we ourselves can't take, but I'm the husband and she's the wife. I call the shots. She owes me fidelity as long as she answers my name and I paid bride price on her head.

I managed with the girls till Saturday then I went to report to my mother.

She was understandably shocked.

"Your wife swore at you with her naked body. Before your children? That is the end of the marriage. It is an abomination. If you take her back as a wife, you'll surely die."

"So we can't be husband and wife again," I was incredulous. "Never!" She spat out. "Not possible again. But what did you do to her?"

I couldn't lie to her, so I told her everything. She didn't blame me.

"You're a man, my son. How many husbands are faithful to their wives? A man will always be a man. She should have overlooked and ignored it. It wasn't even as if you had married the other woman. She was still your only wife."

We talked about how to take care of my daughters. She wanted me to leave them with her but I couldn't imagine not coming home to my lovely princesses. I will keep them and take care of them. I told Mama that Amaka will move in.

"She's a good girl. So she accepted to come into a home with two little children already? She has a good heart. Who knows God may give us a son through her."

We passed the night at our family house. I called Ifunanya and Somto to get ready for departure. They were playing hide- and- seek under the coconut and kola nut trees. I looked up at the trees. No fruits yet. These trees do take some time to mature and bear fruit.

Settling down into regular family life, I soon discovered that the animosity between Ifunanya and Amaka was mutual. They resented each other. How do you reason with a girl who's not quite six, and missing her mother? I tried to make Amaka understand and come down to her level, but she wouldn't listen to me. It pained me seeing my daughter sent to do tasks way beyond her age. She was the plate-washer, errands girl, and sweeper of the house. Amaka called it training, but I called it child abuse. I also saw her verbally abusing my daughter for expressing confusion over her homework. I told both of them to stop doing her homework. I took over teaching my daughter myself. I worried about the hours they spent together from when they returned from school to when I returned from work. When I cautioned Amaka, she accused me of taking sides with my daughter to disrespect her.

Other worrying signs began to show up. Amaka was a poor manager of finances. She was perpetually coming up with lists of frivolous things. She needed jewelry, cosmetics, and hair care. For reasons I couldn't understand, no cream would last beyond one month. Adaugo and I used a giant cup that lasted up to six months. But Amaka was different. Why won't she tidy up her toe-nails and fingernails by herself? Why must she always go for manicure and pedicure? Right after paying my children's fees, she would ask for money for clothes, or wig, or to pay a make-up artist or for jewelry. She would pick a quarrel with me for not considering her a priority. I told her that she wasn't my only responsibility. One day the thought hit me: maybe she had imagined that I was richer than I truly was and she had come to enjoy the money. She had the audacity to ask for a car. Where will I get such money? Comparing her to Adaugo, I saw that the latter had never stressed my life the way Amaka was doing. But I was already caught in a web. Adaugo had left me. If my mother is right, there would be no remarriage to Adaugo. In fact, the effort of her family to make up with us had failed because Mama said she had committed an abomination and I will die if I tried to bring her back. I was stuck with Amaka. Fortunately, I was yet to see her parents. I was surprised that she didn't insist on regularizing our relationship either traditionally or legally. She didn't put any pressure on me to take her to either of our families. It was just as well.

I knew Adaugo was visiting her children in their school. Ifunanya had told me that their mom brought them delicious lunch in their school. I was salivating at her description because Adaugo is a really good cook, but that was enough to throw Amaka into a fury.

"Delicious lunch! So what do I cook for you?" she shouted at the surprised child.

"My mother's food is more delicious," the innocent child was unfazed.

She glared at me to call my erring child to order, but I could only smile inwardly. Which child doesn't think that the mother's food is the best? Let her add it to the list of misdemeanors committed by my daughter and myself. With time, she will learn to loosen up and not get worked up over the comments of an innocent little girl. Maybe when she has a son for me. In the meantime, let us all enjoy the unease which my daughter's speech had brought.

One day I went to pick them from school. There was not much traffic, so I arrived earlier. Then I saw Adaugo. I opened my mouth in amazement. I thought she would have lost even more weight pining for me and weeping over the children. But she had filled out. She was radiant and looked far more confident than I had ever known her to be. I was stunned. I felt the usual desire for her. I had to be careful. Very careful.

As I picked the children I turned on the radio. Was it fate mocking me? It was *Destiny Child*'s song called "Survivor." I listened attentively to the entire lyrics. The song seemed to fit this version of Adaugo that I met. It had an uncanny resemblance to my situation. Like the bluffing artist, now that I was out of Adaugo's life, she appeared to be much better off. I had thought that she'd be weak without me but she was stronger. She wasn't broke without me but comfortable. She obviously wasn't sad or helpless without me but seemed smarter and wiser. Taking the care of the children off her made her look unstressed and radiant. She appeared bent on making her mark in life without me. Troubles had hardened her and inured her from further pain and misery. She seemed not to need me anymore. I had thought that she would be a victim, bemoaning my rejection of her and replacing her with Amaka, but there she was: a victor and not a victim. Adaugo had mastered the art of survival. She's a survivor. I felt a tug of unease. What if there was already another man in her life? Just the possibility was making me miserable.

She looked really pretty. Nobody will believe that she was after two. Haha! She had gone through two pregnancies. Will I blame her if she accepted another lover? Wasn't it my fault that I threw away such jewel to bring in somebody who considered me her money-making machine? I was pensive for a long while after the meeting.

As though the emotional torture wasn't enough, my company was not doing well. Sales of equipment were dropping and management had set targets for staff to generate income. I knew what could happen and I was already hearing talks of laying some staff off. Thank goodness that I had a roof over my head. But Amaka's indiscretion in spending meant that I had little by way of savings. What will happen to us? I was apprehensive about the future. I told the members of my household to manage. The look Amaka gave me showed that expecting such cooperation was vain.

Another thing was puzzling. We had stayed together for about six months and she never missed her period for once.

CHAPTER 16

Alex relives his friendship with Chukwudi

CHUKWUDI AND I HAVE BEEN FRIENDS FROM OUR UNDERGRADUATE DAYS. In life, there is just that special friend that sticks closer than a brother. People gave us names:

"Paul, where is your Silas?"

"You two are like David and Jonathan."

We studied the same course at the university. I was a struggling student and it didn't take me long to realize how intelligent Chukwudi was. He was acing the engineering courses. Occasionally I was torn between admiration for him and pity for myself for not being so sharp. But for him, I would have had low self-esteem even though I was the louder, more sociable one.

I should have just changed subjects at the secondary school level and moved over to the social sciences or arts but my parents would have skinned me alive. They had assigned careers to us. My eldest brother was to be a medical doctor and he was already in medical school. The second brother was to be a lawyer and he was working hard and would soon be called to the bar. My lot was to be a mechanical engineer and that was it according to the law of the Medes and the Persians (meaning my parents) which could not be altered. My petty pride would also not let me change. I attended a co-educational school where it was a source of pride to write Maths, Further Maths, Physics and Chemistry in senior school leaving exams. The girls, many of whom were in the Arts and Social Sciences, admired the Science students and I wanted to belong. You weren't considered brilliant if you were not a science student.

Many who joined us at the beginning of the session dropped off in the middle of the first term to join social science or art classes. I remember Ben's humorous narration of his struggles with Further Maths.

"They warned me that Further Maths would be tough so in the first few weeks, I listened with all the concentration that I could muster. It appeared easy at first and I was happy. Then slowly I couldn't see numbers like 1 and 2 again. Just letters and words that sounded like sine and cosines but I didn't know what they meant. Where was I when the teacher was making the explanations? I hadn't missed any class. And why is the teacher always looking for X? I joined a study group and really tried to make more efforts. Just when I thought it had started making sense and I was making headway, the teacher changed gear. Now he was speaking Greek. Alpha, Beta, Tetha. What were all these? I saw myself rushing to collect an F that nobody was forcing on me. I decided to attend the Government class just to hear what they were being taught. They were talking about the various ethnic groups in Nigeria and what true federalism means. I understood them. It made more sense than those Greek words. I sent for my Mom. There was no point calling Daddy who has always been telling me that I would be a failure. Mommy didn't mind my changing class and I ran from science class with utmost alacrity without looking back."

I couldn't run like Ben. All my elder brothers were already working towards their chosen careers and I wouldn't be the odd one out. My parents often warned us against being the black sheep in the family. I wasn't going to be that black sheep.

I won't disappoint my parents.

My efforts yielded a decent result in WASC and secured me admission to the university. I had thought that passing WASC would be the greatest stress in my life and that university would be for enjoyment and girls. How wrong I was! Engineering Mathematics! Thermodynamics! Maths 101! With shock, I heard that some students carried these courses over into their final year.

The fear of failure can make one humble. I noticed that Chukwudi was brilliant and I attached myself to him. He was my lifeline. Studying with him didn't guarantee me the A's he made but at least I made B's and below and was content.

But all work and no play makes Jack a dull boy. I had my fair share of flirtations and flings like any young man.

We heard about Adaugo and in checking her out, I met Nma too. Two male friends marrying two female friends was the logical thing to do. So we planned on doing just that.

Chukwudi secured a job soon after graduation. Mine came later but with higher pay and better conditions of service. I was uncomfortable telling Chukwudi about my good luck. Life can be so unfair! I was earning better than the person who had taught me, but that's just how it is. Chukwudi was genuinely happy for me and I was relieved.

He got married before me, and I picked the motivation to settle down too. I was still looking up to Chukwudi as my mentor and following his footsteps. I married Nma and we started our family. We visited each other's house and I could see that they were doing great together. Our wives went shopping together, planned birthdays and dinner dates together.

Till tomorrow, I feel sad that coming to my child's dedication ceremony was the beginning of the rift in Chukwudi's household. It was there that he met Amaka. My colleague at work had brought her. Chukwudi and I had been friends for long so I could tell him the truth.

"This girl smells like bad news, Chukwudi. They said a woman's loyalty is tested when her man has nothing, while a man's loyalty is tested when he has everything. Adaugo was faithful to you when you had nothing. As you two are building together, watch out that nothing destroys your beautiful home. I almost fell into this type of trap myself, but my wife helped me. Now I am accountable to her," I had warned him.

He didn't think there was any danger.

"So even if my wife doesn't trust me, you also would not trust me? You know that I love Adaugo. I have always loved her and I still love her too much to cause her any heartache," he assured me.

With concern, I saw the affair with Amaka deepen from an ordinary fling to something more threatening to his family. I sat him down again to talk.

"Don't you think that Amaka " I began

"Do please mind your own business," he shot at me.

"I am a full-grown man who doesn't need you to babysit me. I can make my own decisions. Or is it because you're earning more than me."

The last comment made me doubt if his earlier joy at my job was a cover-up. He must have been envious all the while but he managed to suppress it.

After this altercation, he hardly came to see me. Our friendship went cold. Nma was also having difficulty visiting Adaugo as before. Adaugo never reported him to me. I think she was just avoiding us because she didn't need our pitying eyes. Or maybe she thought that as his friend, we were in each other's confidences and that I approved of his trashy conduct. Amaka became the center of Chukwudi's universe. He was like a bewitched man. He had no more time for his friends. I knew from Adaugo's appearance from the few times we met that she was suffering. Chukwudi avoided me even more. I was watching the crises that engulfed him from both work and home. I remembered the old times; the numerous assignments he had helped me with; our shared joys and sorrows. Without waiting for him to look for me, I reached out to him.

CHAPTER 17

Adaugo is visited by Uche

"Mummy, Dad doesn't put on the generating set at night when there's no light," Ifunanya told me during one of my visits. "Why?"

"He said things are hard. We have to manage."

On another occasion, I met Chukwudi again at the children's school. Why would he come during lunch break? Something told me he intentionally came because he hoped to see me. We still didn't look at each other.

"Mummy, Daddy said his boss wants him to bring customers who will bring money so that they will pay him."

That explained it. He was deployed to the marketing team.

Looks like all wasn't really well.

"Mummy, Aunt Amaka prepared indomie noodles without eggs for us. She said we should manage."

I wasn't on speaking terms with Chukwudi so I couldn't ask him what was going on. It had become normal to meet him on the very day I chose to visit the children. I would have gladly picked a different time, but it was the time my supervisor had graciously approved for me. If anybody was to change, it should be Chukwudi. He shouldn't come doing lunch break and wait till school is over. Or was he having a hard time getting customers?

"Mummy, Aunt Amaka made us soup without meat and fish," reported the ever-faithful Ifunanya.

As we 'accidentally' met again, I looked at Chukwudi. He was losing weight. He was looking stressed. I felt like reaching out to smoothen the creases on his forehead. I turned away quickly and entered my car. People should be left with the consequences of their decisions.

"Mummy, Aunt Amaka has packed out of our house." I opened my mouth but no sound came out.

"Mummy, I didn't ask her to go," my daughter explained. She was harboring the thought that maybe, she was responsible for her moving out.

"Do you know why she left? Did your Daddy tell you?" I asked with a shaky voice.

"No, But after Daddy sold our generator, she was complaining that every time Daddy will be saying no money no money."

I didn't know just how to react, but inwardly, I was pleased with the news. I slept very soundly that night.

That weekend, Uche visited me from school:

"Satan don fall for ground oooo march am march am," she sang.

We were both laughing.

"I heard that your brother's renegade missus has packed out."

"Why won't she? Is God asleep? How can she reap what she didn't contribute to sow or nurture? Whatever is planted on lies cannot thrive," Uche concluded.

"Not every time, my girl. What of all those times when the outside woman succeeded in replacing the madam of the house and heaven didn't fall? Your brother was just unlucky that he didn't get a keeper."

"Your *chi* isn't the same as those people's own."

I agreed with that position. Each scenario was different.

"I think he will soon come to apologize to you," she reasoned. "You think it's as easy as that? You're as vain as your brother.

Do you imagine that I will forgive him and move back despite the insolence and humiliation? Don't worry, I will soon invite you to my wedding to another man." I kept a straight face.

I was surprised to see that Uche believed me. She began to plead with me to forgive her erring brother. I should forget it too. I shouldn't complicate the life of her nieces by having half-siblings and a step-father. She was in earnest.

"Uche, you're begging the wrong person. We are not even sure what your brother wants. He may choose to look for a financially comfortable lady and be a toyboy to her until his finances improve. You're taking it for granted that since Lady Madness has moved out, he will naturally want me back. His ego may not let him beg."

"I don't think so, Auntie." But I had succeeded in curbing her excitement and mine.

"I think that Uncle Nwagbo, who has always liked you, will talk sense to him."

"But he failed in doing that at the beginning of our crisis. There's your mother too. She had threatened to kill herself if I ever went back to him as a wife," I pursued the thought.

"Forget about Mama. Those are empty words. As for all that abomination stuff, all is hogwash. Your future with my big brother depends on what you want."

"Or rather, what he wants," I corrected her.

"It's what you want. I know that he will come to beg for forgiveness. How soon he will do that is what I don't know. But please, Ma, give us time. I know you're still young and pretty. Don't accept anyone else. What am I saying self?" She was laughing as she said the last sentence.

"What's so funny?" Her laughter was infectious.

"I know you still love my brother, so I don't need to beg you to wait for him to come round."

"How do you know? Are you a mind-reader or you're so vain to expect that I can't replace him?"

"It's easy to tell. You love me! I and my brother are one. Even having a doting sister like me is enough reason to forgive and forget."

Uche was always such a pleasant company. We could discuss anything: school life, campus boyfriends and sugar daddies, fashion and career.

It was time to go back to school and I gave her some little money.

"You see why I want you back. You give and give, unlike Lady Madness that came to take and take."

"Goodbye, Uche. We will keep our fingers crossed."

CHAPTER 18

Aunt Winnie stands in the gap

BEING A TEACHER AT A NURSERY/PRIMARY SCHOOL LIKE RICHFIELD School is like following the histories of families. Mothers enroll their first child, then the second, the third, and all others. You follow the children and their growth. Sometimes you become fully enmeshed in their families and their stories. The children also share lots of their laughter and sorrow with us their teachers.

Every good teacher has a favorite child, and it is always the same child: the child who needs us becomes the favorite child. I well remember Erma Bombeck's article on "My Favorite Child." Even though she applied it to mothers, she was describing my job as a Nursery School teacher.

> Every mother has a favorite child. . . . I have mine. That child for whom I felt a special closeness. . . . My favorite child is . . . the child in my arms at the emergency ward . . . the one who . . . misspelled committee in a spelling bee, ran the wrong way with the football and . . . the one I punished for lying. He was selfish, immature, bad tempered and self-centered. He was vulnerable, lonely, unsure of what he was doing in this world . . . and quite wonderful.
>
> All mothers have their favorite child. . . . the one who needs you at the moment.[1]

Ify was my favorite child. She wasn't the most brilliant or the most obedient, but she was adorable. I loved her and came to love her mother too. I still don't understand why it seems that bad things happen to good

1. See Bombeck, "My Favorite Child."

people. From the time Adaugo brought Ify to register in our school, there seemed chemistry, an inexplicable bond between us. I love children and I thoroughly enjoy my job. But Ify's attachment to me was soon noticed by other members of staff.

"Aunt Winnie, your baby is coming," they would announce as soon as she arrived in school.

I think when her mother noticed was when I transferred the affection to her little sister, Somto. Ify would confide in me all her secrets and I enjoyed her prattling.

"Aunt Winnie, my Mommy bought me a new pair of shoes." So we discuss how she wore it to church and which dress she wore with it.

"Aunt Winnie, my Mommy took us to the park. We ate ice cream, played merry-go-round, and water fights."

"Aunt Winnie, my Dad is very handsome and strong." Who am I to doubt her?

I remember on one occasion when she came to the school looking sad.

"What's the matter?" I asked Adaugo.

"I don't know. She said she won't tell me, but that she will tell only you."

My heart was pounding as I took her to a quiet place. What could it be? Rape? Incest? Sexual abuse? I knew from the media how rampant such cases were and I feared the worst. What will this four-year-old not want her mother to hear from her? Adaugo was looking at us, too puzzled to know what to think. I could feel that she was holding her breath, waiting to hear the worst.

Ify and I had our little conversation and I heaved a sigh of relief. I smiled reassuringly at Adaugo and told her to go that it was nothing serious. I had promised Ify that I won't break her trust so I wasn't going to tell her mother right away what the problem was. So Ify smiled and took her place in class.

When Adaugo came for the afternoon school run, she was eager to hear

"Ify told me that she didn't feel like writing numbers one to a hundred today, and that made her sad about coming to school."

We laughed together. Warm laughter of two mothers united in our love for a child.

"So I promised her that I won't worry her. She should write just a little and stop whenever she felt tired." We laughed again!

I thought over Ify's complaint. I don't blame those who criticize our educational system. Should a child of four be made to write so much? Are we not hurrying our children? The school workload is heavy on young children. They are deprived of the privilege of being children. After school, parents arrange extra classes for very young children. By age nine, we have crammed them up and sent them off to secondary school. Some of them enter the university at the age of fifteen. When do they enjoy their childhood? When will they play and discover their world? Why is a school's success measured by how early their children can read and write? Some have said these under-aged children who enter the university are vulnerable and they join secret cults. I don't know how true this is, but I worry about the way we rush children.

I made these observations to my school proprietor, but she told me that if she changed from the norm, she would lose patronage and the school would fold up. So I am forced to make children learn content that is way beyond their age and interest level. To soothe my conscience, I try to come down to the level of the children. I also include a lot of storytelling in my lessons. The children are entertained and hopefully educated too. Generally, they love to come to my class, but insisting on a four-year-old writing numbers one to one hundred was just too much for Ify, even though that was specified in the syllabus for that week.

Ify was brilliant. Her mother was kind. She wasn't one of those mothers that treated their children's teachers as slaves. Some mothers would come to the school and rain abuses on the teachers for the slightest oversight concerning their children. Misplaced lunch boxes or water bottles, wrongly packed exercise books, unfinished meals, minor scratches on the children, or any such was enough reason to storm the school and complain bitterly.

The school management sided with such parents. Nobody will blame the leadership. This is a business relationship and the customer is always right. If they withdraw their children, we will be out of job. The children were pampered and petted like fragile eggs. No physical punishment was allowed. The children could get away with rudeness and insolence. A child in the upper primary once told a teacher that she was so poorly dressed that his mother wouldn't have hired her as a house- help. The teacher wept bitterly and all the remonstrance the child received was that he should watch his language. His mother heard about it and laughed it off as evidence of his childishness.

But Adaugo was different. Apart from occasional tips, she showed concern and respect to the teachers. Her children were also polite and obedient. The other teachers remarked that if the other children behaved like Ify and Somto, we won't have discipline issues at all.

Over time, I began noticing changes in Adaugo and her girls. As she came to drop and pick up the children, there was a far-away pained look in her eyes. She still tried to smile whenever she saw me, but I could sense that she was merely putting up appearances. With time, I noticed that she was losing weight too. Was she terminally ill? What is eating up this once happy exuberant woman? I couldn't pry into her personal life, but I was worried.

Ify had moved on to a higher class and had a new teacher, but they still called me her school Mommy and kept me abreast of her progress. One day her class teacher called me aside.

"Ask your daughter what is wrong with her. Her performance is dropping and she's not paying attention like before."

I sent for Ify during the long break.

She told me that she doesn't know what the matter is between her Mommy and her Daddy. They were always arguing over Amaka and the arguments were making her afraid. She doesn't know who Amaka is, but Mommy doesn't like Amaka.

Ah! That was it! An extra-marital affair! The innocent child is bearing the brunt of the indiscretion of an adult. Does the father know how this sensitive child is taking the tense environment in her home? Beyond paying her school fees and providing feeding, is he aware that his frivolity was having repercussions on this brilliant child? My thoughts shifted to Adaugo. What exactly do I do to help her in this scenario? How do I support a fellow woman whose life is being torn to shreds by the intrusion of another woman in her home? Pitying her will be more humiliating, so I kept up my cheerful front whenever I met her. I confided in Ify's class teacher so that we both could give her the emotional support which she obviously wasn't getting from her embattled mother.

The morning Adaugo packed out must rank as one of the worst days of my life. I knew she had parked out, because, for the first time, Ify's father brought her and her sister to school. I looked at the man and I couldn't control the bitterness and revulsion that I felt towards him. So this is the irresponsible fellow causing this damage to these innocent souls! I felt like physically attacking him, but why should I be the outsider weeping more than the bereaved? What could be his excuse? Did he want a son so desperately after two girls that he couldn't wait? His wife was fertile. They could have more children. Was the Amaka already carrying his son? Did she give it as a condition that Adaugo must get out for her, the carrier of the Almighty male child and heir, to move in? When will we Africans grow beyond this mentality of prizing a male child? So Adaugo didn't matter because she was yet to have a son? And the happiness of these two angels wasn't important either? I wept at how unfair life is. What of the x and y chromosomes they taught us in Biology that shows the male is the determinant of the sex of the baby?

It's infuriating that even educated men still behaved like their ancestors in issues like this. I knew that the man was educated. But he still blamed the woman for having daughters and chased her away to bring in someone that will give him sons. I know a family member who separated from his wife who had three daughters and married a lady who had told him she was pregnant for a son for him. Two years later, no pregnancy, no son. A university lecturer refused to pay his wife's delivery fees. Her offense was that she gave birth to her fourth baby girl. If she had tried hard enough, she would have had a boy, but because she was unfortunate in life, she gets only girls. Horrible attitude! I was angry! Angry at the mindset of my brothers. If education doesn't change them, what would? Have they not seen very successful women who were taking good care of their families?

It occurred to me that I was pre-judging the issue. I hadn't heard from the man and I jumped into conclusions. But I couldn't wrap my head around what else Adaugo could have done. So lovely and concerned about others. Her only fault, as far as I could see, was that she had two adorable daughters. When some people are praying to experience parenthood, no matter the sex of the child, others are throwing away their child's mother for giving them girls. Even when they have not reached menopause. Looks like the man had concluded that even after twenty pregnancies, all Adaugo could ever have would be girls.

I looked at Ify's gloomy face that morning. Her teacher had brought her to me during the short break. What she told me was a nightmare even for an adult like me.

"Mommy called me and Somto into the room where Daddy was. Then she removed all her clothes. Even her pants. She cursed Daddy and Amaka for a long time. Then she dressed up, put her things in her car, and drove away."

My heart was bleeding as I imagined the scene. I was crying and she was crying too. Was this not too much for a five-year-old to take? Couldn't Adaugo keep her little ones off her misunderstanding with her husband? Why did she overreact? How will the children get over this? Who am I to decide for people how they manage hurt? Maybe that was her only outlet for ventilating. But still . . ..

"Why didn't you and Somto follow her?"

"Daddy said No. He said we must stay with him. He dragged us away from her."

I pondered on the decision for a while. How will a working man keep two girls under ten and take good care of them? How will he bathe them, help them with school work, and prepare meals? I was sure that the man was having psychiatric problems. He should have allowed them to go with their mother. Anyway, I was sure the law courts will award Adaugo custody of her children. She should get that quickly before her randy husband would begin to sexually abuse them.

On second thought, the courts may not grant her petition. Her husband will cite her stripping naked as an instance of her not being mentally capable of taking care of her children. If he's able to prove that she's mentally deranged, they may not grant her custody. So much confusion. And the Amaka who caused all these must be rejoicing that her scheme was working. I comforted and encouraged Ify. I told her that God will bring her parents together again so that they could all be one happy family again. I shared her story with her class teacher and we agreed to be praying for God to re-unite this broken home. I tried to find out from Ify if she knew where her mother went to, but she didn't know.

A few days later, Ify brought fresh news.

"Aunt Winnie, Aunt Amaka has moved into our house."

My heart sank. So the outside woman has legalized her stay. She has taken over. So this was the basis of the man's confidence in making his wife leave. He had perfected plans of replacing her with his mistress. But how will this impostor take care of children that are not hers?

I kept watching over Ify and Somto. If they don't know peace at home, the school should be a sanctuary for them. Soon, all the pupils knew that if you bullied Ify and Somto, you will see Aunt Winnie's red eyes. Stories circulate very quickly. Soon other teachers got to know about the crisis in Ify's family and formed a shield of protection around the two girls. It was almost as though they were orphans. They often came to school with their homework undone. Rather than reprimand them, the teachers created extra time to work with them. Their grades were not affected.

One day, I saw a silver lining. Adaugo came to visit them during a long break at school. You could hear Ify's shriek of joy from a mile off. They were tears in my eyes again as I saw mother and daughters in a joyous embrace. We the teachers pretended not to notice her. From the windows of our classrooms, we saw her weeping over her daughters. Then she brought out food flask and gave them food. They had finished their sumptuous meal when the bell rang for the end of the break. Naturally, Ify ran to share her happy news.

"My Mommy came. She brought delicious chicken and rice for Somto and me. She promised to come often to see us."

I was happy for her.

"Did she tell you where she stays?"

"She's with grandpa and grandma. I asked her when she will come back home and she said later. I asked her about Aunt Amaka, she said I won't understand yet."

From then, Adaugo became a regular visitor to school during lunch breaks. I noticed that she was adding weight. She also seemed more confident. She was changing clothes too. Wearing really nice clothes. Serves her husband right. But I became concerned again. Is there a new man in her life? Was she moving on? Is this home irretrievably broken? Adaugo isn't ugly. She had gone through only two pregnancies and was still as fresh looking like any young lady. Men will still find her very attractive. Obviously, she wasn't the cause of the collapse of her marriage. But inasmuch as I wanted her to be happy, I would prefer she reunites with her husband. That was always my prayer. It appeared she was now going out with another man or even other men. Ify's teacher answered my unasked questions.

"Aunt Winnie, we were talking about occupations in Social Studies today. Ify told the class that her Daddy is an engineer while her mother works with the media."

Thank God. I was relieved. She has a job and is picking her bills. It doesn't mean there could be no other man in her life, but if she's financially independent, she wouldn't be rushing into another relationship in order for a man to meet her financial needs.

I was wishing Adaugo back to her home. Ify was telling me all the stories of abuse going on in their home. Amaka made her run errands way beyond her age and ability. She won't help them with their school work. She was also verbally abusive. She taunted them that they were just as foolish as their mother. She was saying hurtful words to little children. It was apparent that the father was trying his best to protect them. She told me how her father quarreled with Amaka over her hurtful words. My heart softened towards him a bit. I didn't know he loved and cared for them that much.

From the quality of food being packed for the girls for lunch, I knew that all was not well financially with the man. From chicken and rice to indomie noodles with eggs to plain indomie.

"Daddy says there's no money," Ify told me. "Aunt Amaka is always quarreling with him over money."

I mentally thanked Adaugo for bringing them good food during their lunch break. They were guaranteed one good meal a day. This went on for several months.

One day, I noticed that their father arrived earlier than usual. Adaugo was still around when he drove in and parked. I was uneasy, but nothing happened. Adaugo quickly entered her car, waved the girls good-bye, and sped off. He waited until school was over and then took them home. I was wondering which man had so much time on his hands. Ify explained.

"Daddy is to look for customers for his company."

So he was now a marketer too. An engineer turned marketer. The organization couldn't be doing well.

My connection with Ify was like literarily living with them. "Aunt Winnie, Daddy has lost his job!"

That was horrible. The food they brought to school was worse than ever. Their socks had holes and they were looking really unkempt. How will this family survive? Adaugo continued bringing lunch. Their father was coming to their school even earlier than usual. He and his estranged wife were meeting in the school more often than before, but nobody saw them talking to each other.

How quickly things had changed! The man was looking lean and haggard; his wife was glowing with health and contentment. Such a transformation! The forlorn woman of a few months ago was replaced by this confident working-class lady holding her head high. The formerly dictatorial haughty man was walking about with a frustrated look. We were watching how it will all end.

One day, what I had been expecting to see happened. "Aunt Winnie, Aunt Amaka has packed out of our house." Ify's teacher and I jubilated over this news.

"God is not asleep. How can someone come, balance, and eat the fruit of your labor?"

It was a very good sign. But will Amaka's exit be automatic reconciliation? Will Adaugo forgive or has she been hurt to a point of no return? Will she go back and pick the pieces of this broken man and work with him and for him to rebuild what they once had? Can the humiliation and shame be forgiven and forgotten? Can healing still happen?

One eventful day, I noticed that Adaugo and Chukwudi arrived at the school at about the same time.

From my window, I noticed that he spoke. And she responded! From the window of my class, I continued observing. Was he laughing or crying? I couldn't tell. They entered her car together with their children. My joy and excitement was like watching a brand new wedding ceremony. Ify's teacher came to my class. She had been observing too. She had tears in her eyes. We were giggling like two teenage girls and talking in whispers.

This is hope. Living breathing hope.

CHAPTER 19

Chukwudi and the test scare

SOMEONE ONCE QUIPPED, 'WOMEN ARE NOT TO BE UNDERSTOOD. THEY ARE to be loved. How can you understand what was created when you were sleeping?' I couldn't understand Amaka. She had told me that she loved me and I believed her. I treated my wife like rubbish because of her. Now that she had achieved her goal of staying with me, she was not satisfied. She was perpetually demanding for money.

As the imminent shake-up in my organization was hanging like a dark threatening cloud, I saw that she was not perturbed. Then I noticed other things. She would receive a phone call, and move away from me to answer it. She put a password on her phone and when I demanded to know it, for the phone I bought for her, she asked me why I was feeling insecure. She would move out of the house to visit her friends without telling me. When I confronted her, she would tell me she's not legally my wife. I told her she owes me faithfulness and she sneered: "So says a husband who chased away his wife because of a mistress. Am I your wife?"

This exchange hurt to the core. She noticed and apologized immediately but the damage had been done.

I had targets to meet at work and a tough environment at home. I started underperforming. It was difficult getting customers and convincing them to buy our products. I needed to be in the right frame of mind before I could transfer my enthusiasm to potential customers. I tried to cut down on our spending but I was faced with the inevitable. We were downsizing and I knew that I hadn't met my target. During the quarterly evaluation, I knew what was coming. I lost my job. I felt like I had been run over by a truck carrying cement.

I told Amaka. I expected understanding and sympathy. She just told me coldly, "well you must try and get another job."

I told her that I was happy that she wasn't pregnant yet. As it was, we had only the two girls to worry about. That was when she dropped the bomb

"Yes. It was good that I was on contraceptives." It was as if I had been dealt a mortal blow.

"You were on contraceptives without carrying me along? I thought we agreed that you will have a son for me."

"You thought I will have a child for a married man who I am not married to? What do you take me for? You want to eat your cake and have it! How will I play second fiddle for you when I can easily be a first wife somewhere? When you asked me to take you to my family did I agree? Do they even know that I'm with you? All they know is that I'm staying with a friend in town while seeking for a job."

I was too dumbfounded to speak. I needed to know everything, especially where I stood with her. So I encouraged her to continue. She told me that she had a fiancé who was trying to raise the money with which to marry her. She had lied to the man that she was staying with her mother's brother in town helping him to take care of their young children. Keeping Ifunanya and Somto lent credence to her story that the uncle's wife traveled out of the country and that she volunteered to help her care for her children. She sometimes let their chatter filter into the background while talking with her fiancé on the phone. So why did she choose me? I asked her. I looked like I genuinely liked her. So she never loved me? No. Love ended with her first campus romance. As far as she was concerned, men were only a means to an end: she needed their money, they needed her body. Period. To drive home her point, she asked me to consider if I would have encouraged my younger sister of her age to go and play a second wife for a married man instead of marrying her own husband. She insisted that I would never have supported my sister.

Each sentence brought its pain and shame. I had destroyed my family for nothing concrete. She explained that her fiancé was the one she was hiding to pick his calls. She would intentionally break at intervals to talk to Ifunaya and Somto to convince him that she was really babysitting.

After her revelations, she moved out. I couldn't stop her even if I wanted. I no longer had a job so my usefulness as a source of free money had expired.

In my solitude, I had the leisure to reflect on my actions. Looks like I was the one who paid the greatest dividends for my actions and choices. I had lost my beautiful family. Adaugo who I genuinely cared for had slipped out of my hands. It now didn't make sense that I cheated on a woman I didn't want to lose with another woman I never planned to keep and who eventually refused to be kept.

I had lost money too. Amaka required maintenance. Every Naira I had spent on her for food, gifts and drinks, I had subtracted from savings that I could have invested in my family's future or at least put more food in my children's mouths.

I had wasted time and time is money. If I had spent the time I had invested in Amaka pursuing a certification course in my field, I would have been assured greater job mobility.

I had also lost respect. Neighbors looked at me in a quizzical manner. I heard people curse me and abuse me as a foolish man and woman 'wrapper.' My siblings were uncomfortable in my presence. They were just respecting me because of my age, but some conversations stopped abruptly as I entered. Eventually, I lost everything: both wife and girlfriend. Talk of losing both home and away matches! After losing my wife, my money, my time, Amaka still left me to begin another life.

Mercifully, my children were still too young to understand. I could read love and adoration in their eyes and that was a huge comfort. If ever I pulled through this, I was going to make it up to them by being the best and most responsible Dad ever! It would have been painful seeing and hearing them dishonor or disregard me. If Ify was up to fifteen years of age, how would I have explained my extramarital affair to her? How would I have justified replacing her mother with another woman? How would I have controlled her if she brought a young lover home?

I had heard of men who were worth nothing before their children. The adulteries hurt the children almost as much as their mothers. They felt their mother's humiliation keenly and despised their fathers.

I heard of how a son discovered the father's adulterous past and confronted him with it. The man had become old and needy and his son was in a comfortable position to cater for him. In confronting his father, he insisted on a new and full apology to his mother and his siblings instead of maintaining a moral grandstanding while being a recalcitrant adulterer. It took the intervention of family members to calm the young man. I could only wince at the thought of being dubbed an irresponsible man in my old age. If I manage to recover my home, I don't believe there's any fling or thrill that I can trade for my family again. They're my legacy and my real source of joy. I had nothing to show for the emotional energy and resources I had spent on the relationship with Amaka.

I remembered an anonymous story I had read somewhere about the dynamics of power in the family.

The writer identified three stages of power in the typical Nigerian family: the formative years in which power rested with the fathers. He had total dominance and was the lion of the house; the indisputable and unchallenged boss who ruled with an iron fist. He barked out orders and determined what happened in the home. He also meted out punishment to the children who grew up to fear him instead of loving him. Some Nigerian men, like myself, threw their adulterous activities in their wives' faces, after all, we could do anything and get away with it. I was the provider.

But power doesn't last forever. As the children grew up, power shifted to the mother. When the children started earning their own money, for some reason, it was their mothers they would decide to look after. They were closer to them because while the father was in charge, he was busy with the business of providing. He didn't have much time to be a friend to the children. They spent more time with their mums and invariably grew closer to them. They also saw their mum as co-victims of the fathers' tyranny. The mother took center stage at this point. She was the first to know what was happening with the children and she had the advantage. If any of the daughters gave birth, she was the one that went for babysitting and the children spoilt her with gifts. At this stage, the father would be wishing for some bond with the children as they have with their mother but that boat had since sailed. Even the mother was no longer dependent on the man for her financial needs. By the last dispensation, power has shifted to the children. They are self-sufficient, live on their own, and have their own families. More often than not, whenever there was a quarrel between father and mother, the children sided the mother. Years of joint victimhood would be at play. Children have been known to come to the house to warn their father not to 'disturb' their mother. If the father's finances were precarious at this stage, he would be humbled by force. The gang-up was real.

Fortunately, my daughters were still too young to understand. Again, I had taken them off their mother. I hope that will soften their hearts if they ever get to know about my treatment of their mother.

My thoughts went to Adaugo again. I truly loved and admired her. How could I have run the risk of rubbing my adultery in her face? Looking at it in retrospect, I felt like a fool. What if she had hired thugs to beat up Amaka? The scandal would have been worse than the one I was presently into. What if she had become so hardened or bitter that she decided to poison my food? Only an autopsy would have revealed the cause of death, but will autopsy restore my life? What if she had become destructive? 'Hell hath no fury like a woman scorned.' She had so many options for revenge. She could have started to cheat on me with other men and would have been so discreet that I would never have found out, or done anything if I did discover.

But she did the honorable thing: she gave me space or rather spaces. She gave me physical space and she also gave me psychological space to sort out my emotions and loyalties. She didn't continue to throw herself at me or force me to love her and live with her. Her absence made me miss her quiet but dependable ways. I came to cherish a woman who was invested in me and the home we were building together. All of these I had lost. I had traded fidelity and solidity for disloyalty, infidelity, and frivolity. My tryst with Amaka was a wildfire which burnt itself out. Underneath, there was no connection. She wasn't my soul mate and I had accorded her emotions which weren't mutual. I had imagined a future with her, but she envisaged momentary pleasure. My soul mate was my ever faithful Adaugo and I had thrown her away. Her affection was the rope, the strong rope around my waist.

I was plagued by another thought: my health. I had been having unprotected sex with Amaka whom I'd come to realize had multiple sex partners. I had foolishly believed that she loved me and was faithful to me. Why did our paths cross? What, in the name of Providence, brought Amaka my way? How did other men survive, knowing that the girl they were cheating on their wives with, owed no one any loyalty or fidelity? I had joined in swimming in a public swimming pool. I had a queen in my life, but I had traded her for a piece of bread. I regretted my actions. I wished I could bring back the hands of the clock. I had to know about my health status. With shaky feet, I dragged myself to the health center where they were offering free HIV/ AIDS screening. A pleasant nurse took a sample of my blood.

The fifteen or so minutes it took for the rapid test result to come out were the worst in my life. I thought of many scenarios: if negative, I can go back to Adaugo and woo her again. I will put whatever effort and take whatever time to secure her regard and start my family again. If positive . . . hmmm . . . suicide. No! I shouldn't even consider that. I was out of a job, so how will I afford anti-retroviral drugs? I will be at the mercy of donor organizations. The panic the thought generated made me rush to the toilet.

I felt a bit better. The nurse was walking towards me. Her face was blank.

"Your test result is indeterminate," she said.

"What does that mean? Why is it not positive or negative?" One could hear the pounding of my heart.

"It means the result is unclear and the test needs to be repeated."

I got up and fled. I raced to my house. Now, this was getting scary. What did I do? What have I done to myself? Just a little straying and I found myself in this shit.

I spent the whole night tossing on my bed. By morning, I had pulled myself together. I needed to know the worst. Not knowing was a lot more agonizing. I headed to another hospital. I had seen this hospital and it looked like they had better equipment. I avoided the hospital that Adaugo had our daughters. I survived the twenty-minute' wait between when they took my blood sample and when the nurse brought the result.

"Congratulations, Sir. Your test result is negative. You are a very responsible man. Please keep being faithful to your wife." I was ecstatic! I had been given a new lease of life. I forgave even Amaka. I thanked her mentally for not destroying my life with HIV/AIDS. I smiled inwardly at the nurse who had called me a responsible man. If only she knew! I was already rushing to my car when she called me back.

"Even though the result is negative now, you may still repeat the test in three months."

I drove straight to an eatery to celebrate my survival. I didn't have much money, but I bought myself a chilled can of malt drink.

I was hopeful and happy once more until my thoughts went back to the sorry state of my finances and home.

There was no money to sustain my daughters and me. I was desperate. I had sold the generator. I sold more items in the house. Feeding was getting tougher. I had no one to leave the children with after school. Sometimes I would lock them inside the house and rush out to do *kabukabu* with the car.

But there was Adaugo looking resplendent. My friends had told me about her job with a media firm. They must be paying her well. I needed her desperately, but how do I approach her? There was no ego to brag about. Can we really not be married again? Will she ever forgive me? Even if she forgives, can she forget?

Ifunanya told me about her visiting days and time. I planned my visits to coincide with hers. But she won't look in my way or talk to me. How do I break this barrier? I have to brave it. For my children's sake. For the past we shared. I preened myself.

One day as she finished talking with the children beside her car, I walked up to her. I thought she would run, but she didn't.

"You didn't even bother to greet me, Adaugo," I heard myself saying.

That wasn't what I wanted to say! I have started off wrong again. With an accusatory tone. She will hiss at me and walk away.

"Since when did we start greeting," she responded.

Joy that I didn't know was possible swept through me. She could still talk to me. But it was joy mixed with huge doses of sadness at the unhappiness which had enveloped us both.

"I'm suffering, Adaugo. I'm really suffering." Without planning it, I burst into tears.

Those who think men shouldn't cry don't know anything. Tears are therapeutic. With each loud sob, I felt the ache, the humiliation, and the pain dissipate. I looked at her. She was weeping too. She opened the door of her car and we sat inside. Our daughters sat in the back seat, watching us cry. It was a healing session. At length, we stopped, and as if on reflex both of us looked at our daughters and laughed. They joined in the laughter. I had not heard such a happy sound in a very long while.

"Where is your Madam Amaka?" She asked me.

'She's gone with the wind. The opportunist has gone to look for other prey. I don't know whether it was juju she used . . .'

Adaugo stopped me. I should have known better. She doesn't believe in all that black magic. I was responsible for my choices and actions. I apologized.

"I'm sorry for the choice I made which brought us so much trouble. If you can forgive me, we can start afresh, please." I was desperate.

"What shall we do about your mother who said it's an abomination for us to still be married?"

"Forget about my mother! There's no abomination anywhere. We shall live together as husband and wife and nothing will happen. In fact, since we didn't do a church wedding before, we shall go for a marriage blessing. We shall also do a high court wedding. You must be my legally, traditionally and religiously wedded wife. God of the Christians has more power than any idol that will strike a hurting woman dead for being angry with her husband. The people I disappointed are your family members. I don't even know how I will face your parents and siblings. I will have to marry you afresh before they can agree for you to come back to me."

I started crying again. I complicated my life. How will Adaugo's family trust me again? But let me secure her regard first.

"What's the price I should pay, Darling? I want you back in my life." I was pleading.

"I don't want us to make our children orphans," she began.

"I understand you perfectly. I have done HIV test. The result is negative. If you're not satisfied, I can do another one. We can hold off normal relations until you're good," I explained.

She started crying again. Even without saying a word, I understood why. It was the image of me with Amaka. I knew that the scene must have been playing and replaying in her subconscious.

"I'm sorry, Darling. As long as we both live, it will never happen again. Give me another chance. I have learned from my mistakes. We have both suffered."

"But they say 'once a cheat always a cheat,'" she countered.

"I don't know how people come by that. But this husband wants a brand new beginning. It is no cheating; no beating."

She looked at my unkempt appearance. I told her everything about the circumstances that led to the loss of my job. She was sympathetic. But then she said "Maybe it's because you're so stressed financially that you came back to me. If you still had your job and money was flowing, you may not have come back. You can't trust the loyalty of a poor broke man."

That was very painful. I wanted to retort, but I held myself back. Didn't I deserve any ill-treatment, abuse, or doubt? How can I expect her to give me her full trust when I had broken it so shamelessly before?

"You may have every justification to think that way, but it's not true. It took Amaka's unfaithfulness to me to open my eyes. I realized I had thrown away a most precious jewel to acquire a fake trinket. Do you remember when I told you the children were ropes tying you to me? That's wrong. The love which we share for each other is the real rope."

Without dwelling on details that will hurt her further, I told her what Amaka had revealed to me. She was shocked.

"She hurt me so much that I felt like reporting her to you."

She laughed and it felt good. Imagine reporting your girlfriend to your estranged wife!

By the time we were done planning our reunion, the school compound was empty. I didn't need to ask her for money. She opened her purse and showed me what she had and we shared it. She went back to work and I went home with a happy heart and grinning children.

CHAPTER 20

Chukwudi makes up with his in-laws

I DREADED VISITING MY PARENTS-IN-LAW. AFTER MY TRENCHANT ATTI-tude when they came to my village to beg, I didn't know how to face them. But before bringing my family members to plead, I needed to clear the ground. I didn't want to see two of them together during my first visit. Adaugo and I agreed that I should begin with her mother, Nkechi. She helped me to determine when only her mother would be at home.

With a pounding heart, I knocked at their gate. Adaugo's mother opened for me. When she saw who it was, she beat a hasty retreat. But quickly I put my hands around her and wouldn't let her go.

"Chukwudi, please carry your trouble and get away from my house."

"You're my mother and a mother doesn't reject her son no matter what."

I don't know where the tears came from, but I found myself weeping. She was touched and calmed down. I knelt and apologized to her. I told her I wanted a brand new start and that she should help me beg the only father I have, that is Obuora. I told her that since the death of my father, he was the only man who ever treated me like his son.

"Please, Chukwudi, stand up," she pleaded.

"Not until you say that you have forgiven me. Don't call me Chuk-wudi. Call me son."

"How can I call the person who nearly killed my daughter, son?"

"Let's forget the past. This is a new son," I was earnest.

"So hardship and poverty reset your brain. Maybe if you become rich in the future, you will act worse than you did in the past. I don't know how Adaugo can choose to trust you again."

I had anticipated this. I would have imagined the same if I was in her shoes. But I was ready to be humiliated or abused provided I had my wife back.

"It's only time that will convince you of the truth, Mommy. I have learnt my lessons in a bitter way. Give me another chance to prove myself. Adaugo knows that I foolishly strayed. It won't happen again." I was still begging.

At length, she softened and we agreed on a date that my family will come for a reconciliatory visit. Three of us came: my mother, Uncle Nwagbo and I. It was like doing the traditional marriage all over, except that we were all sober. We all could recollect when it was her family that visited mine at Okiti. How soon things had changed! Adaugo had given me the money to buy a live goat and other presents with which to appease her parents.

After the uneasy pleasantries, Uncle Nwagbo cleared his throat.

"My in-law, I know that you are a good Christian and you read your Bible well. Here I bring you the real-life prodigal son. He has changed. He is asking that you receive him as a son again. Experience, they say, is the best teacher. After carrying water and oil, you'll know which is heavier. I know that he acted very foolishly, but even God forgives us when we repent and ask for mercy. Forgive and forget."

As he was rounding up, I was already kneeling in front of Adaugo's parents.

"Dad, please trust me again. Forgive my insolence," I was almost choked with emotions.

Mr. Obuora looked away from us. After a long silence, he looked at me and heaved a sigh.

"You offended me. I trusted you with my precious daughter but you betrayed that trust. But my pain is nothing compared to the one you caused your wife. If she's ready to forgive you and continue with the marriage, who am I to stand in her way."

He sent for her. As she arrived, our eyes met.

"Adaugo, Chukwudi is here with his mother and uncle. He hurt me, but he hurt you more. As much as I will want you to be married, I want you alive and happy. You're an adult and I can't decide for you. What do you want to do?"

Before she could answer, my mother started talking.

"Ada m, you may think that I don't like you, but that is not true. I accepted you right from when Chukwudi brought you. Please, forgive me for the role I played in your separation. I was just a mother siding her child. I had said my son would never marry you again, but I withdraw that curse and pronounce that it shall be well with you and my son. Forgive me and take me as a mother as you have always done."

I joined in the begging. I was about to kneel for her when her father stopped me.

"You don't need to do that here to show us. How you treat her later is what will show if you're truly sorry or not."

Uncle Nwagbo joined in:

"Ada, we love you. Sometimes people don't value what they have until they lose it. Thank God that we didn't lose you first before knowing your worth. I have never known Chukwudi as a philanderer. Just once that he tried what others are doing recklessly, and he nearly pays for it with human lives. Forgive. Come back to your home and continue building with him."

We waited for her to speak.

"I am ready to go back to my home. But Chukwudi has to promise you people here that there will be no cheating and no beating," she said.

"See, Darling, if at any point I raise my hands over you, move out and never come back. If you discover any infidelity, walk out too," I promised before the family.

They asked us to hug each other. I didn't stop at hugging her; I kissed her.

Uncle Nwagbo presented the gifts we brought.

"My in-law," he addressed Adaugo's father, "we can't thank you enough for taking care of our wife for the long period that she was with you. We know that she's your daughter, but you had married her off to us, so she is our responsibility. We brought these little tokens to thank you and your wife for a job well done. We can see that she's looking healthy and happy."

He presented the goat, some fabrics, and cartons of soft drinks.

We ate and drank together and I took Adaugo back home. I had prepared the girls for their mother's return, but the excitement was way more than I could ever have imagined.

I had advised Ify to avoid any mention of Amaka's name to her mother. When it slipped out of her mouth, she turned to me with an uneasy look. Adaugo was wondering why the chatty girl suddenly stopped talking.

"Daddy said I shouldn't mention Aunt Amaka to you," she explained.

But Adaugo hugged her close.

"Feel free to tell me everything and anything," she reassured her.

JUST THE FOLLOWING MONTH AFTER HER RETURN, ALEX GOT ME A JOB IN his company. That was all I needed to set in motion the things I had planned.

"Darling, we are doing a court wedding next month," I informed her.

Somto and Ify leaped for joy.

"Daddy, Somto and I will be your flower girls!"

"Of course yes."

I saw that Adaugo was happy. I heard her talking excitedly with Nma about bridal wear and bouquets and veils. I was happy that I could make her happy again.

On the set day, Alex, Uncle Nwagbo, and my Mom accompanied us to the High Court. Adaugo's parents came and signed as witnesses in the marriage register. We were legally married and my wife now had conjugal rights. We came back to a simple home-made meal which she and Nma had prepared.

But I wasn't done.

"Darling, we shall have Church blessing for our marriage," I informed her.

"Daddy, another wedding? How many weddings shall we do?" queried Ify.

"Don't you want to be a flower girl and march into the church?' I asked her.

"We want!" Somto responded even faster than her.

This took even more planning than the court wedding, but my wife was glowing with love and joy. I overheard Nma teasing her.

"Maybe my marriage should scatter first so that Alex can court me afresh."

Adaugo's face clouded.

"I'm sorry. I was just joking," Nma beat a retreat. "It's just that I admire how Chukwudi is wooing you afresh and pampering you. Who doesn't like a better thing." She thawed and they laughed.

Simple as it was, a lot of planning still went into it. Finally the day came. I had told the priest that I will like to take the full marriage vow. Finally I could promise my wife that I will be her lawfully wedded husband, to have and to hold, to cherish and to protect, to keep myself for her and for her alone until God by death shall separate us. I could appreciate the full meaning of the vow. There was a finality about our relationship and an understanding that we had no alternative than to remain married to each other.

I looked forward to the day I will hold Ifunanya's hands, and later, Somto's, as they stood beside their husbands taking similar vows.

CHAPTER 21

Adaugo gives birth

"Mommy, your tummy is big," Ifunanya said.

"I'm going to have a baby!" She was happy. Somto was happy too.

"It's going to be a girl." Somto said. "I want a little sister."

But the scan result had shown a boy. Chukwudi had begged me not to ask for information about the sex during the scan. He didn't want anything that will upset me but he didn't know that I had gone past the level of being upset by such things. I would gladly have welcomed another girl after the turbulence in my marriage. What mattered most was that we were happy together.

Chukwudi was also doing so many things he wasn't doing before. He shared his phone password with me. I told him it didn't matter, but he said he wanted zero secrets. He wasn't ready to go through another merry-go-round in the hands of any schemer. He wanted to be fully accountable to me.

As I returned to my matrimonial home, good returned. Alex had heard of Chukwudi's job loss from a mutual contact. I was to learn later that after Amaka left him, he made up with Chukwudi who was now clinging to him for pressing financial needs. He knew that it wasn't dignifying giving him financial support, so he did only what was absolutely necessary. When there was an opening for contract staff in his office, he pleaded with the HR manager to allow him to bring a friend to fill the position and she agreed. That was how Alex helped Chukwudi to secure another job. It was paying slightly less than what he had been earning but we were so glad that he had a job.

He insisted on my being a joint signatory to his account. It looks like what nearly tore us apart had the effect of bringing us together more powerfully.

He would call from work to tell me how much he loves me. He arranged lunch dates and family outings. He remembered my birthday and our numerous anniversaries: we celebrated the date he came to my school, the date of our introduction, the date of our traditional marriage, court marriage, and church blessing. Not elaborate outings, but he remembered everything that had to do with our shared history and which strengthened our bond. I was glowing.

The birth of our son was hitch-free and joyous. My husband named him Udochukwu (God's peace).

After his dedication, we visited his mother. There stood the coconut and kolanut trees. Both trees were in full bloom and the seeds, the pods, were coming out in full strength.

Bibliography

Bombeck, Erma. "My Favorite Child." *My Inspired World* (blog), May 22, 2007. http://myinspiredworld.blogspot.com/2007/05/my-favorite-child.html.

Gass, Bob. "Are You Feeling Like a Victim?" Cited from *The Word for Today Daily Devotional*, by Bob Gass, April 7, 2011. https://pttyann2.wordpress.com/2011/04/07/are-you-feeling-like-a-victim/.

www.ingramcontent.com/pod-product-compliance
Lightning Source LLC
Chambersburg PA
CBHW060811250626
47162CB00005B/1740